"How did you think to take the boy home?" the man asked.

"Why, on the donkey," Elizabeth answered, surprised.

"A woman alone?" he asked. "All that way?"

"I came alone," she answered, looking at him directly. Then she realized what he had said: "A woman alone." She had not thought of herself as a woman, but only as a girl, Caleb's sister. The blood rushed to her face. What must this man think of her, alone here at night? Bowing her head, she murmured, "Surely with my little brother no one will harm me. And there is no other way."

Also by Edith E. Cutting

Deborah of Nazareth

ELIZABETH
Of Capernaum

EDITH E. CUTTING

DAVID C. COOK
PUBLISHING CO.

David C. Cook Publishing Co., Elgin, Illinois 60120
David C. Cook Publishing Co., Weston, Ontario
Nova Distribution Ltd., Torquay, England

ELIZABETH OF CAPERNAUM
©1991 by Edith E. Cutting

Designed by Richard Schroeppel
Cover illustration by Rick Johnson
First Printing, 1991
Printed in the United States of America
95 94 93 92 91 5 4 3 2 1

Cutting, Edith E.
        Elizabeth of Capernaum
        1. Marriage—Fiction. 2. Jesus Christ—
Fiction. I. Title.
PZ7.C9953De   1991
ISBN 1-55513-948-5
Fic—dc20   91-10898
                                            CIP
                                            AC

For Becky Daniel whose inspiration and
encouragement helped bring these books into being.

1

ELIZABETH HAD JUST FINISHED laying the last of the fish on the drying rack. For the past two years, since she was eleven, she had worked with other girls and women for the owners of a big fishing boat in Capernaum. Her father, who had only a small boat, was glad of the few coins she earned each day. She was quick and skillful as she scaled and cleaned the fish and laid them open to the hot Galilean sun. This morning as usual the boats had come in soon after sunrise, but they had been only half full.

"Elizabeth! Elizabeth!" She heard her name being called and lifted her head. Her mother was hurrying along the rough bank toward her.

"Be careful, Mother! Don't fall."

But the older woman paid no attention. Now she was trying to run down the stony beach. "Elizabeth, is Caleb with you? Have you seen him?"

"Caleb?" she asked. "He was still asleep when I left."

"I know. When he woke up, I gave him his breakfast, and he went out to play. I thought he might be with you."

"Could he be with Amos? They're usually together." Elizabeth began wiping her hands on the cloth at her waist.

"No, I asked there first," her mother answered. "Amos is playing alone, and his mother has not seen Caleb. Oh, Elizabeth, I'm so worried."

"I'll go look around," Elizabeth said comfortingly. "The fish are done for today. There wasn't a very big catch. . . . Have you asked Rachel?" she added, thinking of her older sister.

"Oh, you know Rachel," her mother answered fretfully. "She doesn't have eyes for anybody but Adam lately." Then she began on another worry. "If his father doesn't speak for her pretty soon, I don't know what she'll do. You know last night she almost burned the fish for supper. She was looking right at them and didn't even see them begin to smoke."

Elizabeth laughed. "That's my big sister. She'll come down to earth when she and Adam are married."

Elizabeth and her mother were already climbing the bank, and Elizabeth's mind turned back to her little brother. "How long since you saw Caleb?" she asked. "Did he say where he was going to play?"

"No, I just told him not to go far, as I always do,

but I was putting the beds out to air and then grinding meal—Elizabeth, I'm so afraid."

Elizabeth slid her arm around her mother's waist. "There's nothing to be afraid of, surely. He can't have fallen into the water. If he'd come down here, I'd have seen him, or some of the other women would have."

"But Elizabeth—" Her mother shivered. "There was a caravan outside the village last night. You know where they stay."

The two stopped to let the older woman catch her breath. "Caleb wanted to go see the camels, but I said no. His father was out with the boats, and the camp is no place for a woman."

"Where's Father now?" Elizabeth asked as they started on toward the house. "Does he know?"

Her mother shook her head. "He was going to take his fish on to Tiberias this morning. He said the market was better there. Oh, Elizabeth, what if he comes home and Caleb is not here?"

"Well, we'll certainly find Caleb before he gets back," she answered hopefully. *No wonder Mother is shaking,* Elizabeth thought, remembering times when her father was in a temper. "Maybe Caleb's home now."

But when they got to the house, there was no sign of the little boy.

"You stay here," Elizabeth said, "and I'll go over to the caravansary. If he went there, somebody must have seen him." Quickly she picked up her black scarf and flung it around her shoulders.

"But you should not go there," her mother objected weakly.

Elizabeth gave her a quick hug. "I'll be all right. The caravan must have left by now. Caleb may not be sure which way to come home. I'll find him."

Neatly she rolled up a small loaf of bread and some figs in a clean cloth. "He'll be hungry before we get back." She smiled at her mother and hurried out.

"Caleb!" she called as she ran along the road. "Caleb, where are you?"

Once or twice she stopped to ask a woman who came to a door whether she had seen Caleb, but nobody had. At the last house before the caravansary, she had better luck. "A little boy about five?" the woman asked. "I did see one, but I thought he belonged with some of the camel drivers. I noticed his light hair, though. He had on a blue coat—"

"That would be Caleb," Elizabeth said in a tense voice. "But where is he now?"

She ran on to the field where the camels had stayed, and pounded on the door of the inn. When a man opened it, she panted out her question. Had he seen a little boy this morning? A little boy about five?

The man scratched his head. "I don't know. There might have been, but I was too busy to notice." He called his wife, and she came to stand just back of him.

"Yes, there was a little boy. I noticed because they don't usually have children with them," she said. "He asked if he could have a ride, and one of the drivers laughed and said, 'Why not?' "

"But where is he now?" Elizabeth interrupted. "Even if they gave him a ride, they must have put him back down. Didn't they?" she insisted. She grew pale as she asked again, "Didn't they put him down off the camel?"

The man shrugged and turned away. "We've got too much to do to watch your children. If you'd kept him home the way you should, he'd be there now."

But the woman took time to whisper, "I don't think they put him down. They were leaving toward Jerusalem—"

"Wife!" the man shouted from the back of the inn. She turned and scurried after him.

Elizabeth felt sick. What to do now? How long since they had started? Probably soon after sunrise. She turned away, calling "Caleb! Caleb!" again, just on the chance he was somewhere near.

If her father had gone to Tiberias, he would not be back till afternoon or evening. It would be too late then for him to follow the caravan. Maybe he would not even come home, but just go out fishing again for the evening catch. And if he came home and found that Caleb, his only son, was lost . . .

Elizabeth caught her breath. *I must go after him*, she thought. *I'll need a donkey. Uncle Levi will let me take his.* She knew Uncle Levi could not go after Caleb because he was blind, but he still had his donkey. Elizabeth turned and started running down the side road toward the house where he lived with his daughter.

When she got there, she found him sitting in the shade of the acacia tree, with his cane in his hand. "Uncle Levi," she panted, "can I borrow Thistle? Caleb is gone and I have to find him."

Her uncle grunted. "He can't have gone far. Have you looked around the village?"

"I've called and called, and the woman at the caravansary said he was there this morning before the caravan left. Please, Uncle Levi, I have to go after him."

Uncle Levi frowned. "A girl your age should not go off by herself. Where's your father? And anyway, a donkey can't catch up with camels. They don't look as if they go fast, but they do."

"Please, please, Uncle Levi. Father is in Tiberias. The camel train is only two or three hours ahead. I'll ride Thistle as fast as I can without hurting him. Part of the time I'll walk and let him rest. I won't stop to eat. I'll just give him a drink and go on. The caravan will have to stop sometime, and then I'll catch them. I have to find Caleb, Uncle Levi! He'll be afraid, alone at night with strangers."

Uncle Levi's hand tightened on his cane as he stood up. Then he slapped the cane against the trunk of the tree. "If I could only see," he said angrily, "I'd go, but . . ." He shook his head. "All right," he said at last, in a worried tone. "Keep your scarf over your head." Then his face softened and he smiled at her.

"It's a good thing you always liked Thistle. Rachel was afraid he'd bite her."

Elizabeth laughed with relief and raced around back of the house. Quickly she saddled the donkey. She gave him a piece of bread, tied her parcel on the saddle, and jumped onto his back.

As she started him toward the road, she called out, "Thank you, Uncle Levi." Then she pulled up and stopped the donkey. "Uncle Levi," she called again, "will you go tell my mother? Tell her I'll bring Caleb back in the morning." As she started on, she added under her breath, "If I can just catch up with him tonight."

Elizabeth patted Thistle on the neck and kicked his sides a little to hurry him on. She would have to go as fast as she could now while he was fresh.

As he settled into a steady jog trot, Elizabeth's spirits began to rise. Surely she would find Caleb before night. This was the first time she had ever been out of the village alone. The whole family had gone to Jerusalem for Passover, of course, so she knew the way. But then she had been walking and talking and singing with all the others.

Now she had time to look around. How graceful that soaring eagle was! Elizabeth smiled to herself. Too bad little Thistle didn't have wings. It would be a lot smoother ride. She looked at the low, branching olive trees and the red and yellow anemones among the rocks.

As the day advanced, the sun shone down hotter on her head and shoulders. It was a good thing she had brought her scarf when she dashed out of the house.

If she just didn't have to worry about Caleb, this would be fun. Galilee was such a beautiful country! She hugged herself as Thistle went pattering along. The Sea of Galilee was beautiful, too, of course, but she did get sick of looking at those fish every morning.

Elizabeth lifted her face to the sun. Surely the Lord made all things beautiful—even the fish, she thought ruefully. She really could not blame Caleb for wanting to ride on the camel. She had always wanted to ride on one herself. If only she could find him all right and get him home again safely. . . .

Soon after noon they came to a well where she drew water for Thistle and herself. She remembered having stopped here before, on the way to Jerusalem. But there was no time for memories now. As soon as Thistle had finished chewing his half of the bread, they started on. Elizabeth walked for a while, leading the donkey down a sloping part of the road. But when it was level again, she climbed onto his back and started him into a trot.

By late afternoon she was getting tired and worried. Suppose she didn't catch up with them tonight? There were jackals in the woods. And hyenas. She tried to shake off the thought. After all, they could not reach her when she was up on the donkey. But suppose Caleb wasn't with the caravan after all? Maybe she should have looked around the village more. *Too late to worry about that now,* she thought. Then an even more scary thought came to her: Suppose the caravan went down through Samaria instead of crossing the Jordan the way she knew? Her family had never gone that way because there were brigands in the forests there. Elizabeth sat up straighter. She could follow the tracks if the camels turned off that way. And robbers—they wouldn't bother with just one donkey.

Still uneasy, though, she slid to the ground and hurried along leading Thistle. There was nothing to do but keep going and stop fretting.

The sun slid down behind the hills, and the shadows began to get darker. At a little brook, Elizabeth let Thistle drink again, and they ate the last of the figs.

Then she began to run, pulling the donkey along till he trotted faster. She wasn't used to running far and, before long, felt a pain in her side. Stumbling over a loose stone in the path, she fell flat. Thistle stopped and nudged her to stand up.

2

"OH, THISTLE, I'LL HAVE to ride again," Elizabeth said, almost in tears. "You would not fall over a little stone like that."

She climbed into the saddle and started on again, with Thistle walking this time. "Little Thistle, what would I do without you?" she whispered. Somehow she didn't even want to talk out loud. She felt so alone, and yet afraid someone might hear her there in the dark.

The night breeze began to come up, and the trees seemed to be closing in over the path. Still the little donkey kept plodding along. Once Thistle got too near a thorn tree, and it ripped Elizabeth's sleeve, leaving a long scratch down her arm.

Nervously she kept patting Thistle's neck as she watched the moon rise over the trees. Would he keep going all night? Or would he just stop? Then what would she do?

Suddenly Elizabeth lifted her head. She had caught a whiff of something on the breeze. Was it smoke? Could it be the smell of camels? Thistle broke into a trot. He must have smelled something, too. Did he think he was going to be fed?

Elizabeth held her head high, turning this way and that. There it was again. Just a whiff and it was gone, but Thistle seemed to know where he was going. Then Elizabeth heard a faint sound of bells. Maybe a camel had jingled them as he lay down. "Hurry, hurry, Thistle," she whispered.

The road seemed to be curving through the woods, but at last, far ahead in an open space, she could see little fires where the men must have cooked their supper.

Thistle settled back into a sedate walk, and Elizabeth leaned over to lay her face against his neck. "We did it. We did it," she murmured to him. Then she jerked up again. They had found the caravan, yes, but what about Caleb? Anxiously she slid to the ground and hurried ahead, pulling on Thistle's bridle.

Suddenly a hand seized her arm. "Who are you?" a man demanded. "What are you doing here?" He gave her a rough shake.

"Oh, is Caleb here?" she gasped. "A little boy? Did he come with you?"

The hand relaxed a bit. "What do you know of a little boy?"

"He's my brother. Caleb is his name. He was lost, and we thought he came with the caravan." She tried to twist her arm away. "Is he here?" she cried. "Caleb!"

A hand clapped over her mouth. "Don't wake every brigand in the country," the man muttered. "I'll take you to the master. Will you be quiet?"

She nodded, taking a deep breath. As he dropped his hand, she whispered, "Where is he?"

Still holding her arm, but not answering, he turned toward the end of the caravan where several men were sitting by the coals. "Leave the donkey there," he said as he began to pull her along toward the others.

At the fire he explained briefly. "This one just came from the dark. She says she is the little one's sister. I will go back on watch." He turned and left silently.

Elizabeth fell to her knees. "Please, please, where is he? Caleb, my little brother."

The men just stared at her. "Is he safe?" she pleaded. "He is with you, isn't he? Please, is he all right?"

Curtly the leader spoke. "Are you alone?"

"Yes, yes," she answered. "He was lost and my father was away from home, so I came. Please take me to him. He's never been alone at night before."

With deliberate slowness the man stood up. "You might have given thought to the child before," he said scornfully. "Why was he allowed to be alone at the caravansary? A fine mother you will be!"

Elizabeth bowed her head in shame. What could she say? That she was not Caleb's mother? The man knew that. She had come as soon as she could.

Slowly she raised her head and looked into the

dark eyes staring down at her. "I am much at fault," she said in a low voice, "but please take me to him."

At last he nodded and led her to a little cave beyond the fire. There Caleb lay sleeping, stretched out on a rich saddle blanket, one hand under his cheek as always, but with tearstains down his face.

Wanting to gather him in her arms, Elizabeth held herself back. This was no time to wake him, but tears began running down her own cheeks. Humbly she knelt and kissed the man's hand.

He pulled back quickly. "You will sleep with him," he said abruptly. "Have you eaten?"

Elizabeth nodded. "I had bread and figs."

"When?" he asked.

She could hardly remember. At last she said, "Afternoon, I think. I stopped for the donkey to drink two different times, and we ate them."

"That is not enough," he said. "Come to the fire, and I will get you some milk."

"May I touch him first?" she whispered. "I will not waken him, but—"

With a single nod he turned away.

Elizabeth crept into the cave and knelt beside her little brother. Soft as a butterfly, her fingers touched his feet, his arms, a lock of hair. *He's all right!* she exulted silently. Not a scratch nor a black-and-blue mark anywhere. At last she rose and went back to the fire.

"I would not trouble you," she said. "I will only sleep and leave early in the morning."

"Eat," he said gruffly, and she saw he had provided not only the camel's milk, but cheese and bread as well. Suddenly in relief she felt as if she were starving. As she sat down, he walked away and squatted with the men by another fire.

When she had nearly finished, he came back to her. "It's a good thing we stopped early," he said, "or you would never have caught up. How did you think to take the boy home?"

"Why, on the donkey," she answered, surprised.

"A woman alone?" he asked. "All that way?"

"I came alone," she answered, looking at him directly. Then she realized what he had said: "A woman alone." She had not thought of herself as a woman, like her mother or Rachel, but only as a girl, Caleb's sister. The blood rushed to her face. What must this man think of her, alone here at night? She reached to pull her scarf closer around her shoulders and realized it was not there. Bowing her head, she murmured, "Surely with my little brother no one will harm me. And there is no other way."

He said nothing, so she went on in embarrassment. "I had a shawl, but I think I lost it when I fell."

"Is that what happened to your arm?" he asked. "You were not attacked?"

"Oh, no." She glanced down and realized that where her sleeve was torn the long, red scratch showed underneath. She tried to pull the sleeve together. "There were thorn trees," she explained.

Again he simply nodded and said, "Sleep now. We shall see in the morning."

She rose and thanked him, then turned and went to the cave. Silently she lay down and cuddled near her little brother, making sure she did not waken him.

It seemed only minutes before he wakened her. "Lizabeth, Lizabeth," he was saying. "You came. I knew you would come," he added bravely.

Quickly she squeezed him in her arms. "Oh, Caleb, Caleb, why did you run away?"

"I didn't run away," he said. "I just wanted to ride on a camel, and the man said I could." He stopped and then went on, "But it was a longer ride than I wanted."

Hastily Elizabeth stood up. It was hardly light yet, but she could hear the camp beginning to come to life. She shook the saddle blanket and folded it. "Oh, poor Thistle!" she said. "I forgot to feed and water him last night. Stay here," she told Caleb. "I must go see to Uncle Levi's donkey."

She hurried out of the cave and looked around to find him. There he was, tethered to a tall, slim tree and munching calmly on a pile of grass. She ran to the donkey, and as she did, the man she had talked with last night appeared beyond him. "Where can I get water for the donkey?" she asked.

He looked sternly at her as he answered, "He has already had water. You forgot him last night."

"I know," she answered humbly. "Thank you for

taking care of him." She petted Thistle's nose. "He is a good friend. He will take us safely home."

"No," the man answered. "I will take you home."

"Oh, no," Elizabeth protested. "You have the whole caravan to see to. They cannot waste time waiting for you to take me back. We will start directly and be home before nightfall." Gratefully she looked up at him. "You are most kind, but—" She stopped. There was a funny little twist to his mouth. Was he angry? Or laughing at her?

"Are you managing this caravan, or am I?"

Again Elizabeth felt the blood boiling up into her face and bowed her head to hide it. "You are, of course," she murmured. "I did not mean to contradict but only—"

"Well, then, this is what I plan," he interrupted. "I have a racing camel that I am taking south with me. Her load is light, and we will divide it among the others. They will complain, of course, like all camels. . . ." His face lightened as he grinned down at her. "But I can get you and Caleb to Capernaum and be back with the caravan before tomorrow night."

Elizabeth looked up, her eyes sparkling. "You mean—we can all ride on the camel? Oh, I've never ridden on a camel." Then her smile disappeared. "But what about Thistle? Uncle Levi's donkey? He can't keep up, but I must take him back. I promised Uncle Levi I would take care of him."

"Many a caravan is led by a donkey. You and Caleb

will ride on my camel, and I will ride on the donkey so she will follow me."

Elizabeth started to laugh, but quickly covered her mouth.

"And what objection do you have to that?" he asked, and added under his breath, "Little camel!"

"You are so tall," Elizabeth said, still smiling, "and the donkey is not very big."

He smiled back at her. "The camel is tall, and you are not very big, but we shall manage. Come, eat now, and on the way home you shall tell me how this whole thing happened."

Elizabeth hurried to get Caleb from the cave. One of the men snatched up the folded blanket and headed for the tallest camel, which was lighter colored than the others.

They broke bread quickly, and Caleb was still munching a piece when the tall man brought them to the kneeling camel. "Her name is Keva," he said. "And yours?"

"Elizabeth," she answered. "My father is Ezra bar Laban, a fisherman on the Sea of Galilee." She looked up at him with a question in her eyes, but he answered before she could ask it.

"Nathan," he said. "Nathan bar Judah, and my home is in Jericho."

Easily he helped her onto the camel and lifted Caleb into her arms. "Hold tight to the saddle post with both hands," Nathan told her. "A camel isn't nice and even, like a donkey. She will pitch you ahead and then back as she gets up. Caleb, hang onto your sister's arms." He stepped back and spoke to the camel.

Suddenly Elizabeth was thrown forward with a jolt, but she held tight to the post with her arms on each side of Caleb as Nathan had told her. Then up came the camel's front, and Elizabeth began to laugh. "She gets up like an old lady," she called to Nathan, and he laughed and turned to the donkey.

3

BY SUNRISE THEY WERE WELL on their way, and Elizabeth had gotten used to the sway of the camel. "It's almost like Father's boat when the waves go under it," said Caleb.

"Yes," she agreed, "and you keep holding on so you don't get thrown overboard."

"Will the fishes bite me?" he asked with a giggle.

"No fish here, but I'll bite your ear if you don't sit still."

Ahead, she saw Nathan stop the donkey and slide off. He scooped something off the bushes and handed it up to her with a smile before they started on. Her shawl! "Oh, thank you," she called, but he was already back on the donkey leading the way.

The sun was high beyond the hills, and she was glad of the scarf to protect her, when they came to the well where she had stopped the day before.

Nathan made the camel kneel, then lifted Caleb down and reached his hands up to her. The camel groaned as she slid down, and Elizabeth laughed. "Were we that heavy?" she asked.

Then more soberly but with her eyes shining, she said, "That was wonderful. You are so lucky to have such a beautiful camel. I never thought I'd get to ride on one."

"Did you mind her motion?"

"Mind?" asked Elizabeth in surprise. "It was fun." She reached out her hand to touch the camel as she would have petted Thistle, but Nathan pulled her back.

"She's not a pet," he said sharply. "You're a stranger, and besides she even tries to bite me sometimes. Stand away now."

He was unfastening a bag from the rear of the saddle, and Elizabeth called Caleb to her. "Come help me draw a bucket of water," she invited as she hurried to the well.

"The camel was watered this morning," Nathan called to her. "Just draw enough for the donkey."

"And us," added Caleb. "I'm thirsty." They sat on the ground to eat and said no more till Elizabeth and Nathan were finished and waiting for Caleb. Then Nathan said, "Tell me now, how it happened you left the child alone."

"I was cleaning fish for drying," she said, with her head bowed. "He was asleep when I left the house."

How could she go on? She could not blame her mother. It was Caleb. She turned to him. "Why did you go to the caravansary, Caleb? You know you aren't supposed to go there."

"I just wanted to see the camels," he said. "And I asked politely if I could have a ride, and the man said I could."

So he was the one to blame! Now she was angry at Nathan. She turned to him with her eyes flashing. "Why did you let him? You could see he should not be there."

"Not this man," objected Caleb. "He didn't know. He just yelled to start, and the other man didn't have time to take me down. But I hung on tight," he added.

"Abdullah was very wrong," said Nathan quietly, "but he has a boy about Caleb's size, and I suppose he was lonesome. Each camel has its place in line, so he had to go. I didn't see the boy till we had left Capernaum far behind."

"He stopped the whole caravan for me," Caleb interrupted with pride.

Sternly Nathan turned to him. "Why did you tell me your home is in Jerusalem?"

Caleb's smugness collapsed, but he answered, "My father says every Jew's home is Jerusalem."

Abruptly Nathan burst out laughing, and shakily Elizabeth joined in. "Out of the mouths of babes," Nathan said at last. "Come, we must be on our way. I thought he had been left behind and I would be returning him home, but I didn't expect to be doing it in this direction."

As they stood by the kneeling camel, Nathan turned again to Elizabeth. "Would you feel better riding the donkey, or do you still want to ride with Caleb on Keva?" He smiled. "I know which one he prefers."

"Oh, I would not change," answered Elizabeth, "unless you want me to. Ever since we started this morning I've pretended I'm going to Damascus or—" she took a deep breath, "or maybe Baghdad or Alexandria." She smiled up at him. "Even the names sound exciting, don't they?"

Nathan did not answer but stood looking at her seriously. Her smile faded. "But of course I will ride on Thistle if you would be more comfortable on Keva. Or really, Caleb and I can ride Thistle all right from here, and you can get started back."

His eyes held hers, and they stood silent. She had forgotten what they were talking about, when he said, "No," stiffly and reached out to help her onto the camel. "I will stay with you till we are in sight of Capernaum. Then I will turn back, and you can ride safely home with your rescued brother and tell your family only what you wish."

Elizabeth laughed. "You are not counting on Caleb. Do you think he will keep still about his great adventure?"

Nathan handed Caleb up to her, and they started

on. As he had promised, he stopped before the camel would be seen and they traded places. He stood watching till they were well started, then mounted his camel. When Elizabeth glanced back, he was already swinging swiftly into the distance.

They rode directly home, and Elizabeth stopped only long enough to leave Caleb, with his mother weeping and laughing and hugging him, while she went on to Uncle Levi's. There she stopped to tell him all that had happened and thank him again and again for the donkey.

"I couldn't possibly have caught up with them if it hadn't been for Thistle. I know I rode him too fast and too long, but I did stop for water, and he's not lame or sore. I'll rub him down now." She stood up at last.

Her uncle spoke gently. "And you, little one? Are you lame and sore?"

Elizabeth smiled ruefully. "A little. But I'll be all right as long as Caleb is home—and I don't think he will try that trick again."

Late that afternoon Elizabeth's father sailed into port to have supper before going out for the night's fishing.

He was in good humor, having sold both days' fish for a better price in Tiberias. "It just takes some business sense," he told his wife smugly, as he caught up Caleb and set him on his knee. "And how has my son been doing?" he asked.

"I rode on a camel!" Caleb burst out. "And I stayed all night and rode back on it. Her name is Keva."

His father laughed. "And I suppose she flew through the air, to get you home on time?"

"No, really, I did ride on a camel," Caleb insisted, "and Elizabeth came and brought me home."

Puzzled, his father looked at Elizabeth, Rachel, and their mother. "What's he talking about? Did you take him over to the caravansary?"

His wife shook her head. "He ran away, and I could not find him." She began to cry, so Elizabeth picked up the story.

Her father listened in amazement and growing anger. When she told about taking her Uncle Levi's donkey, he burst out, "You, a child, to go off like that? What was he thinking of?"

Softly Elizabeth answered, "He was thinking of your son, Father." His arms tightened around Caleb. "Uncle Levi would have gone, but you know he could not have seen. And I have ridden his donkey before."

He nodded, but then demanded, "Why weren't you watching him as you should have been? Why did the caravan leader steal the child in the first place? I'm not a rich man, able to pay a ransom."

"He didn't steal me, Father. He didn't know I was there till we had gone a long ways."

"Yes," agreed Elizabeth, vexed at being blamed after all she had done, "and then Caleb, the little donkey, said his home was in Jerusalem. They thought he had been left behind and were going to take him there."

Still wanting to blame somebody, her father held Caleb tight but turned his fear and anger on the others. "Three women, and you can't keep track of one child!" he shouted. "Suppose my son, my only son, had been hurt or killed and not come back? I've a mind to beat the lot of you."

His wife threw herself onto her knees. "My husband, do not, I beg of you. He is my son, too. If he had died, you could have killed me and welcome. But he is alive, and one of your daughters risked her life to bring him back."

He grunted. "She should have thought of him earlier. Her life is only a burden to me. Two daughters and only one son. And Rachel not yet spoken for."

Realizing that the worst of his temper was past, his wife stood up and hurried to the hearth. "I will cook the fish you brought, and Rachel will make new bread. Elizabeth, run to the garden and bring fresh leeks and cucumbers. Our son is alive! Let us rejoice and be glad."

The sabbath began at sundown that night. The next day the whole family went to the synagogue. They usually did anyway, but this time they went especially in thanksgiving for the deliverance of Caleb.

Elizabeth loved to listen to the readers. Sometimes they discussed parts of the Torah, but sometimes they just read the rolling verses till they sounded like waves and wind on the Sea of Galilee. Sometimes they read the stories of their people—Abraham and Isaac, or

Moses. She smiled as she thought of the story of Joshua and Caleb coming to this land. Sometime she must ask her mother if Caleb was named for that man.

Now she edged to the front of the balcony where she could see the men below. She breathed a prayer of thanksgiving to God when she saw little Caleb close by his father. The man who was reading the scroll was younger than usual. She had not seen him before.

He had read clearly and powerfully and begun to talk about what he had read when a loud voice broke in. "What do You want with us, Jesus of Nazareth?" A man came lurching and stumbling forward, shouting as if possessed by a demon.

Elizabeth shrank back, but could not take her eyes from him. Some of the men tried to reach out and hold him, but the rabbi waved them back and spoke directly: "Be quiet! Come out of him."

Elizabeth caught her breath as she saw the man fall. He twitched and groaned, but then he lay still. Was he dead? No, he was getting up slowly and looking quietly at the rabbi.

But the service had been disrupted, and people were talking and pushing and crowding around. "Come," said Elizabeth's mother. "We will go home to be there when your father comes. He will know what happened and what will be done about it. Such a disgraceful scene! Right in the synagogue."

The stairs were crowded with women chattering and questioning, but they finally got down and walked slowly home. There they laid out the special food for the Sabbath and waited.

When Caleb and his father finally came, they were as excited and confused as the women had been. "Did you see the man fall down?" asked Caleb, jumping up and down. "He was sick, but he got all better."

His father nodded, looking at his wife, "He was as calm as you or I when he stood up. I had thought he was drunk at first, but it must have been a devil in him. The men say this fellow has been raving out in the countryside for days. I never knew a rabbi could command evil spirits." He sat silent for a moment, then added, awestruck, "But this man did."

Breaking off a piece of bread, he held it in his hand. "They say he's from Nazareth, and he teaches by telling stories. I'd like to hear him sometime when there's no trouble. I wish he hadn't been interrupted today, and yet—I would not have believed if I had not seen."

4

In the next days Caleb was never allowed to go out by himself. Even when he went to play with Amos, his mother took her sewing or spinning and sat where she could see him.

"I'll be good, Mother," he promised. "I won't go to the caravansary again."

"You certainly won't," his mother agreed. "If I have to tie you to my skirt, you will never go there again."

The days went by calmly. His mother was so busy with the housework that she could not follow him every day. Some mornings he went with Elizabeth when she went to the shore to work on the fish, and once in a while his father would let him go on the boat.

The fishing was not good that season, and soon it was clear that Elizabeth would no longer be needed at the drying racks. She was worried, because she knew her mother did not need both her and Rachel to help in the house, and the family did need what little money she could earn.

One day her father came back from taking his catch to Tiberias. One of the merchants who usually bought some of his fish had asked if he had a daughter who was a good worker. His mother was becoming more and more palsied. She needed somebody to work for her, but she didn't want somebody from Tiberias who would gossip about her all over the city.

"I told him I had a daughter who could keep her own counsel, and I would bring her the next time I came." He leaned back against the wall, looking at Elizabeth and Rachel. "I don't care which one of you goes, but certainly your mother doesn't need two of you here to keep one house."

"Tiberias," faltered Rachel. "I'd never get to see—" She covered her mouth with her hand and looked beseechingly at Elizabeth.

Elizabeth's face brightened. "I'd like to go," she said. "I've never been anywhere but Jerusalem at feast time. What is Tiberias like?" she asked, turning to her father.

He shrugged. "Much like Capernaum," he answered. "But Romans come there for the hot springs, so mind you behave yourself with them around. I don't want it said again that any daughter of mine goes running off alone after a caravan."

Elizabeth lowered her eyes. "It was for Caleb—"

"I know, I know. But you just keep to your work and that will fill your time. I'll know if you're not satisfactory. I know what goes on, and don't you forget it."

"Yes, Father," Elizabeth answered quietly. "I will try not to make you ashamed of me."

He nodded. "Well, get your things together. I'll take you on the boat tonight and go right—No, that's not a good idea. I probably would not get a good catch with a woman on the boat. If I fill the boat during the night, I'll come back into port early. You be ready. We'll go down along the shore to land you in Tiberias and sell the fish."

"I will be ready," Elizabeth agreed. That night she spent extra time getting Caleb ready for bed.

"Tell me a story," he asked as usual, so she told him the story of Jonah and the big fish. "Did he really and truly swallow Jonah?" Caleb asked.

Elizabeth smiled. "Yes, but he swallowed him whole and then gulped him up again, so it didn't hurt Jonah one bit."

Caleb relaxed. "Tell me another story," he said, but before she could start, his eyes closed and he was asleep.

"I'll miss you, Caleb," she whispered as she leaned over and kissed his cheek. Then she wrapped the few things she would need in a clean cloth and tied it, ready to go in the morning.

The sun was shining as she ran to the pier with her bundle. She had seen her father's boat coming in. It was low in the water, so she was sure he had had a good catch.

She climbed into the boat, and they tacked away from shore. As the sail filled, they began gliding south.

Elizabeth lifted her face to the breeze. What fun! It was a lot smoother than riding Uncle Levi's donkey, or even the camel. She smiled as she thought of last night's story. The sunshine was certainly better than riding in a fish's belly. Poor Jonah! But he did go to another city after all. She wondered if Nineveh would have been anything like Tiberias.

As they sailed smoothly into the harbor at Tiberias, she half wished they had not gotten there so soon, but she felt excitement bubbling up inside her. What was it going to be like here in a new place? What would the lady be like?

"Wait in the market," her father said. "There's a bench over there where I can see that nobody bothers you. I'll sell the fish first, and then we'll go find the house where you will work."

Elizabeth nodded and climbed out onto the pier, carrying her bundle. The place was noisy and busy as the buyers pushed around the boats and yelled their offers or demands. Farther back were the carts from the country with fresh fruits and vegetables. She would like to have wandered around to look at everything, but she knew her father would worry, so she sat down where he had pointed and waited quietly.

She was getting tired of staying still when her

father finally appeared with a big, square-built man. She stood up quickly. "Here is my daughter," her father said.

Elizabeth bowed her head, but not before she had seen a worried look on the man's face. "You don't look very sturdy," he said, thoughtfully. "Will you be able to scrub and cook and run errands for my mother?"

Elizabeth nodded. "I have done those things at home, and I have worked at the fish-drying racks as well. I am strong, so your mother can lean on me if she needs to."

"Well, we shall see," he said, making up his mind. "Come now. I will take you and your father to the house so he will know where you are."

He turned and strode off through the market, her father beside him, with Elizabeth hurrying along behind. They didn't have far to go, but it was a little uphill, away from the water, and on a side street. Elizabeth smiled as she looked out on the harbor and saw the gulls whirling and diving. It would not be so different from Capernaum after all. She looked up at her father. "I'll be able to see your boat sometimes," she said.

He nodded without looking at her. "Maybe I'll bring Caleb one day," he added huskily. "The Lord bless you and keep you," he said and quickly kissed her on each cheek before turning away.

Without waiting to watch him down the street, she turned to the other man and said, "I'm ready now."

The house was larger than Elizabeth was used to. She glanced around quickly. There was no place for cooking, so there must be another room. She could see a little open courtyard with another doorway or two. Suddenly ashamed to be staring, she turned back to the elderly lady sitting on a low stool. Elizabeth thought of her Uncle Levi. The woman's hands were shaking, and her head was quivering, too, but it wasn't that so much as the anger in her face. She looked as if she hated not being able to do things.

Abruptly she snapped at Elizabeth, "Well, you're not very big." Then looking up at her son, she added, "What did you do—bring me a baby to take care of in my old age?"

It sounded so much like her father's faultfinding when he was worried, that Elizabeth wasn't disturbed at all. Instead, she knelt quickly and looked up into the lady's face. "I'm thirteen years old," she said, "and very strong. If you will teach me what you want me to do, I will be glad."

"Well," the woman answered, looking down at her, "that's different from that last flighty thing I had. What can you do? Can you make good bread? Can you wash clothes without tearing them all to pieces?"

Elizabeth nodded. "My mother taught me those things." She looked calmly into the bitter face. "If you would like me to, I can comb your hair and pin it smoothly."

For a minute she thought she had said too much,

as the anger flared again in the unhappy eyes, but suddenly the woman began to laugh. "Does it look that bad?" she asked, as she put one shaking hand up to it. "It feels bad enough, the Lord knows."

She looked up at her son. "You can go now. We shall get along all right." Then turning back to Elizabeth, she said, "The comb is in that cupboard. Hurry and get it. I can't wait another minute!"

Every day the woman's son brought fresh fish for his mother, with vegetables or fruit from the market. Some days he hurried away as soon as he had left them, but other times he stayed to visit with his mother. When he did that, he often watched what Elizabeth was doing. At first that bothered her, for fear he would not be satisfied. When she got more used to the work and to his coming, though, it did not upset her.

Finally one day, he asked Elizabeth if she were satisfied with her job there. "More than satisfied," she answered happily. "It is like a home, and your mother is most kind to me."

He nodded, approving. "And she tells me you are kind to her. It was a good decision, then." He stood up, touched his mother's shaking hand gently, and left.

Some days, though, his mother wanted something special and sent Elizabeth to the market with a basket and some coins to bring back what she had a taste for.

Those times were a delight to Elizabeth, for she could wander around and see things she had never seen before. There was beautiful linen from Egypt and delicate glassware. Besides the things she saw, Elizabeth liked to listen to people talk, with all their different ways of speaking as they haggled or gossiped or told stories.

Now and then as she looked over the harbor from the house, she would see her father's boat. The first time, she had run all the way down to see him. He had been glad to see her, but after a few minutes she realized he was uneasy because she was keeping him from business. He was irritated, too, because Adam and his father had begun bringing their fish to Tiberias. After Elizabeth had asked about her mother and Rachel and Caleb, she said she must not be away from her work long and hurried back to the house.

One day the older woman said to her, "Why do you never say my name? You are respectful always, but you never speak my name."

Elizabeth blushed and said in a low voice, "I'm sorry. I do not know your name. My father did not say."

The woman stared at her. "You've been here all this time and don't know whose house you work in?"

"But I know you," Elizabeth answered. Then she flushed again. "One day I heard one of your friends call you Susan, so to myself I call you Aunt Susan." Anxiously she added, "I hope you don't mind."

44

The woman smiled and held up her arms to Elizabeth. "Mind? Come here, child. I've never had a niece, but you shall be my first, and I shall be your Aunt Susan. I would call you my daughter, but I cannot displace your mother." Formally she kissed Elizabeth on each cheek, then pushed her away. "My husband was Jonah bar Jonah, and my son has the same name." Then she laughed and added, "So you have been swallowed up in the house of Jonah."

Elizabeth laughed, too, but objected. "I have stayed here much longer than he stayed in the fish."

"And I hope you stay much longer yet," agreed the new Aunt Susan.

Another time Elizabeth was shopping in the market when her father's boat pulled in. Caleb was with him that time, so she took her little brother around the stalls and booths until their father finished his business.

"Father lets me go in the boat many times now," Caleb explained proudly. "He says when I grow up I will be a fisherman like him."

Elizabeth smiled down at him. "And you are growing tall already. See, your head comes way up to my middle. Soon you will be as tall as I am."

Caleb nodded importantly. "Maybe I'll be taller," he announced.

When his father called, he turned quickly toward the boat. Then he stopped and asked, "When are you coming home? I miss you."

Tears stung her eyes, but she blinked them back and smiled again. "Do you?" she asked. "Well, you come see me again. I will not be coming soon because I have work to do, and Aunt Susan would miss me."

"Aunt Susan?" he asked. "Who is she?"

"The lady I work for," Elizabeth explained. "Someday I'll take you to see her."

5

A FEW DAYS LATER Elizabeth's father took Caleb with him again, but the catch was so small it was not worth taking to Tiberias. While he was docking at the wharf in Capernaum, a stranger approached.

"Ezra bar Laban?" he asked courteously.

Elizabeth's father nodded. "That's my name," he answered shortly. Tired and hungry, and angry at his poor catch, he just didn't want to be bothered.

"And this is your son Caleb?" the stranger went on.

"My son, indeed."

The man glanced around to make sure no one else was near enough to hear. Then he went on, "I have only a short time here, but I have been asked to see Ezra bar Laban, a Galilean fisherman having a small son Caleb. I am to ask about his daughter, whether she is promised or whether the offer of a man in business would be considered."

Ezra looked at him in doubt. He had long expect-ed Adam's father to approach him, but he had not done so yet. Who was this? A businessman, he had said. Why wait? Perhaps he was wealthy and would offer a good bride price.

"Run home, Caleb," he said. "Here, take these fish to your mother and tell her we will have a guest."

Then he turned to the stranger. "You will sit at meat with me?"

The stranger bowed his acceptance as Caleb scur-ried away with the fish. "You have a good business here," he said. "A man who owns his own boat can make a good living for his family."

Ezra shook his head. "It is not always so. Today, as you can see, the haul was poor, yet even so I often have to pay to have the fish dried or salted."

They walked slowly up the wharf and toward the house, talking as they went. It would not do to talk business in front of the women. As they approached, they could already catch the good smell of fish broiling over the coals.

When they entered the house, Rachel brought water to wash their hands and feet and knelt to dry them with a rough towel. "You see my daughter," said Ezra proudly. "She is well trained by her mother and no doubt made the bread to go with our fish today."

As she stood up, a little frown gathered on the stranger's forehead. He looked keenly at her, but Rachel kept her face down and said nothing. She helped her

mother set the places and serve the food. Then they
drew back till the men had eaten.

At last the two rose and went to the door. The
stranger thanked Ezra for his hospitality and added, "I
shall talk with my nephew about the matter we have
discussed. No doubt I shall return soon."

Rachel's father extended a gracious invitation and
added the words Moses had from God: "The Lord
bless thee and keep thee."

When he came back into the house, he was rubbing
his hands together. "Ah, my daughter," he exclaimed,
"your future looks bright after all. This man has said his
nephew has seen you as his caravan passed through,
and he looks kindly on you. His nephew travels in a
camel train to trade in the south and east and would
consider offering a camel or its worth as a bride price. I
said it should be at least two camels, but he will return
when he has talked further with the young man."

Rachel was staring at him as he went on. "Of
course the dinner pleased him well, and I told him you
made the bread—which you can do, naturally."

Aghast, his daughter whispered, "You mean I am
to be married to this man?"

"Not this man," her father answered impatiently.
"His nephew, a younger man who wants a wife and is
eager to have it settled."

"But Adam—" she protested. "I always thought—"

"Well, so did I," her father blustered. "Your mother
and his have talked enough, but his father has said

nothing, and we can't wait forever. You'll be able to go to Damascus and other cities, he said."

"Father!" Rachel exclaimed. "You mean I have to ride on a camel and go in the caravan and sleep outdoors—"

"Oh, he said Nathan had a good house, too. I made sure of that. In Jericho," he added.

Rachel had brightened at the mention of the house, but now she sank down on her knees. "Jericho!" she said. "But that's miles and miles away!"

"Well, what of that?" her father demanded. "You didn't think you were going to live in this house all your life, did you? And with a large bride price like that, I'll have more for Caleb when he grows up."

Desperation gave Rachel the courage she didn't usually have, to make one last effort. "I will tell Adam. He—I'm sure he—"

"You will say nothing!" her father shouted. "I know him. He and his father are planning to buy a new boat instead of planning any marriage portion. Here is a chance for a really worthwhile bride price."

Rachel broke into tears.

"Now don't go weeping and mourning around. I've made a good bargain for you. You ought to be grateful. I'll give you plenty of jewelry when I sell the camels. But no, nothing I ever do is right, here in my own home. Wipe up your tears now, and don't let Adam see you looking like a sepulcher or he won't want you either, in case something happens to this offer." He turned to leave the house, kicking a stool as he stormed out the door.

In Tiberias the days slipped by, and Elizabeth was happier than she had ever been before. Aunt Susan was teaching her many things she had not even thought of: how to set the table attractively with mats and flowers, instead of just putting bowls out for everybody; how to bake special little cakes; how to make her hands soft instead of dry and chapped as they had been when she worked on the fish. She was even learning the first stitches in embroidery, though Aunt Susan could no longer hold her own hands still to do it. All the while, Elizabeth kept the house spotless.

One day when Aunt Susan's son came in, Elizabeth noticed that his right thumb was red and swollen. As she took the fish from him, she asked, "How did you hurt your hand?"

"Oh, it's nothing," he answered.

"But it is," she insisted, reaching out and lifting his hand so she could see it better. "Did you pinch it between some boxes? Let me wash it off and put some salve on it."

"No, don't bother," he answered, but left his hand lightly in hers. "It's such a little thing. I got a sliver off the wooden crate of oranges. I tried to get it out, but I couldn't manage my knife with my left hand."

Elizabeth was already wiping it off with a damp

cloth. "I can see it," she said. "Let me get a needle."

While she ran to get one from the embroidery basket, he admitted to his mother, "I thought it would work itself out, but it does stay sore."

In a minute Elizabeth was back with a needle. She took his big hand gently, then smiled at him as she would have at Caleb. "This will hurt, but I'll be quick."

She was quick, opening the flesh above the splinter and then sliding the needle deep under it. "There it is!" she exclaimed as the thumb began to bleed a little. "Now let me wind a cloth around it." She poured a few drops of wine directly into the cut and bound it up.

"A healer as well as a housekeeper," he said with a smile. "Great accomplishments for one so young."

She smiled back, rinsed the needle, and replaced it in the sewing basket.

The next morning the thumb's redness and swelling were gone. "And so is the soreness," he added. "It was clumsy of me to get a splinter in the first place, but you were so deft I thought you would like a sewing kit of your own."

He handed her a little ivory box with a thimble and two needles inside.

"Oh, how lovely," she exclaimed, "but you should not—it was nothing—"

"Not 'nothing' when my hand feels so much better," he said. Then he sat down by his mother to tell her the news from the latest caravan passing through.

After he left, Elizabeth had to show Aunt Susan the

little kit again. "I won't touch it," Aunt Susan said, "for fear I'd drop it, but turn it around so I can see it all." Elizabeth could see she longed to feel it, so she laid it in Aunt Susan's lap, where her trembling fingers stroked it gently. "It makes me think of things in Alexandria, when I was there with my husband."

She sat quietly, remembering. "My husband took me so many places when we were young," she said softly. She talked on for half an hour, telling Elizabeth of the gold jewelry, the dishes, the rich fabrics in the market places, and of the pyramids, those tombs of the Egyptian kings.

The way Aunt Susan talked of the world was new to Elizabeth. At home they had talked of fish or boats or storms on the lake. Now as the days passed, they talked of places beyond the Great Sea, of people Aunt Susan had known, of strange tales her husband had heard in other countries.

They talked of music, and Aunt Susan brought out the small harp she used to play. Her hands trembled too much to play now, but she showed Elizabeth how to hold it and pluck the strings. She was even teaching her a few songs. Though Aunt Susan's voice was thin and squeaky, Elizabeth could catch the rhythm and the words, and sing as she thought it might be.

One morning when she woke early, Elizabeth took her basket before breakfast and hurried down to the market. She wanted to find the grapes Aunt Susan particularly liked, the green ones with the misty bloom still on them. She had just picked up a lovely big bunch when she heard a man's voice beside her. "What are you doing here?"

She turned, and her face shone with joy when she saw Nathan standing there. "Nathan!" she exclaimed, "Oh, I thought I would never see you again!"

His face did not respond. Instead he said coldly, "I take it you did not want to. Is that why you told me your father was Ezra bar Laban of Capernaum? To send me in the wrong direction?"

Elizabeth gasped. "No, oh, no. He is my father, and he does live in Capernaum. And so did I till he said I should come here to work for a lady."

Nathan's face softened, but his eyes were still cold. Suddenly he realized that the stall keeper was listening avidly. "Come outside the market," he said. Then noticing the bunch of grapes in her hand, he gave the seller some coins and turned quickly away. "Come," he said again.

Breathlessly Elizabeth followed. Beyond the gates she saw Keva kneeling patiently as she chewed her cud. "Keva!" she cried. "Oh, I wish—but you said I must not pet her." She stood still, thinking back to the day she had ridden the camel. "Oh, if only Caleb could see her again! He comes sometimes on Father's boat. Perhaps today?" She looked up questioningly.

Nathan shook his head. "I have far to travel today. I stopped only to get some fresh fruit to eat on the way. But tell me," he went on, still puzzled. "I asked my uncle to find your father and—and—talk with him about his daughter. And he did, but he came back and said she was a tall girl, quiet and with a sad face—not like yours."

"Oh, that was my older sister, Rachel," Elizabeth explained. "She is sad because Adam's father has not yet made arrangements for them to marry. But he will," she added confidently, "because Adam cares about her, too."

Nathan's face tightened. "No, he will not, for I sent an offer to marry her."

6

THE COLOR DRAINED OUT of Elizabeth's face as he went on, "I thought since you were young, you might have grown a little taller. I thought it must be you, and if you were unhappy at home, I wanted to take you away quickly."

Then he burst out roughly. "Why didn't you tell me there was another daughter? I would have named you, but I was afraid your father would think you had not been circumspect, to let me know your name." He seized her arm and shook her. "Why didn't you tell me?"

"You wanted to marry me?" she asked in a whisper, looking up at him. "Me?"

"But of course," he answered. "Why did you think—" He stopped as he saw the joy flooding up in her face. They stood silently looking at each other.

Then he groaned as he turned away, wringing his hands. "Oh, Elizabeth," he muttered, "your face is like the sunrise—each day different. Why was I in such a hurry? How can I bear that downcast look the rest of my life? And how will she bear me?"

Elizabeth reached out gently. "Surely we can explain." Suddenly she pulled back her hand and asked, "You are not betrothed?"

He shook his head. "But offered. Offered to Ezra bar Laban's daughter. And it is not you."

Elizabeth took a quick breath. Betrothals were as final as marriage. But he was not betrothed. If she talked to her father? He wouldn't listen, she knew, not with a good marriage for Rachel offered. Adam? No, a girl should not approach a man about marriage. Perhaps Aunt Susan?

"I must be going," she said at last. "Aunt Susan will want her breakfast. When will you be coming this way again?"

He stood still, looking at her. "Not for weeks. Perhaps months. My uncle's business takes me south into Egypt, and who knows where after that."

"Oh," sighed Elizabeth, "how I wish I were going with you." Then a teasing smile broke her seriousness. "At least you cannot be married while you are in Egypt. Perhaps Rachel—or my father—will grow tired of waiting!"

There was no answering smile as he said quietly, "But you will not?"

"No," she answered. "I will not."

She turned and started up the street. She walked

sedately, but just barely kept from skipping. How could she be sad when Nathan wanted to marry her? Even if he was promised. There was time. There must be a way.

It was only a few days later when she saw her father's boat coming into harbor, and she was sure she could see Caleb's head over the rail.

"Aunt Susan," she asked, "would you mind if I go down to the harbor? I have not seen Caleb in so long, and I think he is in the boat."

"Run along, child," she answered. Then she added, "Why don't you bring him up to see me? It's been a long time since my son was little, and I'm afraid there are going to be no grandchildren. I'd like to see this Caleb of yours."

Happily Elizabeth threw her scarf over her head and shoulders and started for the harbor. There were some things she wanted to ask Caleb by himself, and maybe he would not talk about them afterwards if he had the visit in his mind.

When he saw her on the pier, he began waving, and as soon as he had jumped out of the boat, she could see he was brimming with news. She didn't have to ask.

"Rachel's going to be married," he shouted.

"Oh, how nice," Elizabeth answered innocently as he ran into her arms. "Are she and Adam going to live with his father and mother?"

"She isn't going to marry Adam," he answered. "Elizabeth, what's so bad about getting married? She's crying all the time."

"Getting married isn't bad," she said. "It's good to get married and have a little girl or a little boy like you." She gave him an extra squeeze.

"Well, Rachel doesn't act like it."

Elizabeth ignored this. "Who is she going to marry, then?"

"I don't know. It's somebody rich, because Father says she'll have a house and live in Jericho. Where's Jericho?"

"It's near Jerusalem, where we go for Passover. Remember? Maybe Rachel doesn't want to go so far away."

"But you're far away, and you like it, don't you, Elizabeth?"

"Yes, I do, and you will, too. Aunt Susan asked me to bring you to see her today. Would you like that?"

"Will she have some dates or figs? I'm hungry."

Elizabeth laughed as she took his hand, and they started up the hill. "I'm sure she will, and we'll be back in time so Father won't have to wait."

Aunt Susan did indeed have dates and figs both, besides little honey cakes Elizabeth had made the day before. Caleb bowed to Aunt Susan as he had been taught, and sighed blissfully when Elizabeth settled him to his feast. Elizabeth and Aunt Susan watched happily but didn't need to say much to each other.

There was one cake left on the plate when Elizabeth said, "Father will have sold all his fish by now, Caleb. We must hurry back to the harbor. Say good-bye to Aunt Susan."

Caleb looked wistfully at the last cake, then turned to Aunt Susan. "Thank you for the cakes," he said politely.

"You are most welcome," she answered. "Would you like to take one to your father?"

With a big smile, he agreed. "And Mother and Rachel, too."

"Caleb!" Elizabeth scolded.

But Aunt Susan only laughed. "Just like my son when he was little. May he always be as generous. Elizabeth, wrap up the ones that are left from yesterday's baking so he won't spill them on the way. Will you come see me again, Caleb?"

He nodded, clutching the package, and they started toward the harbor.

When Elizabeth got back to the house, she found two ladies who frequently came to call on Aunt Susan. They were talking excitedly, so Elizabeth went into the next room, not to interrupt them. There she arranged grapes and slices of orange on her favorite tray. She smiled as she realized there were no honey cakes to add, but she piled almonds around the edge of the tray for extra nibbling. After offering the refreshments to each of the guests, she set the tray on a low stool near Aunt Susan. Elizabeth had learned to stand in such a way that no one could see her put anything in Aunt Susan's mouth. This time, though, Aunt Susan was so excited she just pushed Elizabeth aside.

"Some other time," she said. "Listen, you come from Capernaum. Do you know of a special rabbi there? Why didn't you tell me he can heal the palsy?"

"I don't know anybody who can do that," Elizabeth protested.

Impatiently, Aunt Susan waved her shaking hands at the other women. "Tell her. Tell her."

"His name is Jesus," one of them said, "and He comes from Nazareth, but He often stays with friends in Capernaum. He is a friend of James and John, the fishermen, sons of Zebedee."

"Does your father know them?" Aunt Susan interrupted.

Elizabeth nodded, but before she could say anything, the other lady went on. "They say He can heal all kinds of sicknesses if you just ask Him. He goes around the countryside preaching and healing people instead of just teaching in the synagogue."

"You mean—" Elizabeth started, looking from the other women to Aunt Susan.

"Yes, yes," Susan said excitedly, her head twitching and her whole body tense, for agitation always made her trouble worse. "I'll go wherever He is if he will only free me of this shaking devil!"

That word reminded Elizabeth. "Oh, I did see Him, once. I remember now. It must have been He. I'm sure my father said that was His name. He was in the synagogue at Capernaum."

She was seeing that incident again in her mind. "A man came in staggering and shouting, and the rabbi just told the evil spirit in him to hold his peace and come out. It was such a struggle the man fell down, but when he got up, he was cured."

Suddenly Elizabeth was excited, too. "Oh, Aunt Susan, if he could only cure you! I didn't know He did it often. I thought that time was something special."

"It was special," agreed one of the women. "I wish I had seen it. But Susan is special, too."

"Does He ever come to Tiberias?" asked the other one.

"I don't believe so," put in Aunt Susan, "or my son would have told me about Him. But I would go anywhere. I could go in a donkey cart or a litter or a boat. Elizabeth, would your father take me in his boat?"

Elizabeth was torn. She wanted to say yes. "But the boat would be dirty and smell of fish."

"I don't care, if I could just get to Him. Ask your father when he comes. Tell him I will pay well. And I'll ask my son to find out where this Jesus will be."

A few days later Elizabeth's father did come. He was shocked, though, at the idea of taking a lady in his boat.

"But Aunt Susan said she would pay well," Elizabeth reminded him. "And I could come down and help you clean the boat after you sold the fish."

He thought a few minutes, looking out to sea. "I'd really like to see that rabbi again," he mused. Finally he shook his head. "I'd lose the next night's fishing, and she wouldn't pay enough to make up for that. I can't be wasting my time during the week. If He's back in Capernaum, I may hear Him some sabbath."

Suddenly Elizabeth's father scowled as he watched a new boat sailing into the harbor. "Why don't you ask Adam and his father?" he sneered. "They've got a new boat. They can buy that even if they can't afford to offer a bride price for Rachel. Well," he said, starting to unwind the rope, "I don't have to worry about that now, anyway."

Elizabeth stood there watching as his boat tacked away from the pier. She had been so sure he would do it. Then her mouth tightened, and she lifted her chin. He hadn't thought she would ask the others, but she would. A boat ride would be so much easier for Aunt Susan than a donkey cart. After all, she had known Adam since they were children. It wasn't like asking a stranger.

She hurried along to where the new boat was tying up and waited till the men jumped onto the wharf.

"Elizabeth!" said Adam. "What are you doing here?" Hesitantly she started to tell him. As his father came and listened, she stumbled even more, but at last she got through the whole story: Aunt Susan's palsy and the new rabbi and the new boat. "Aunt Susan says she will pay well, and I'll help you clean the boat, and bring cushions and rugs for her to sit on, if you only will."

Adam hesitated and looked at his father. Elizabeth held her breath. Would they? Oh, would they?

At last his father nodded firmly. Looking at Adam, he said, "If she'll pay, we'll do it. This boat cost us enough, and if we can get something extra, it will help toward—" He stopped, embarrassed at saying so much.

Adam's face lit up, though. Elizabeth guessed he was thinking of Rachel. "The rabbi is to be in Capernaum for the Sabbath, so He is probably staying a few days at Peter's house. "

His father nodded. "If she wants to come tomorrow, we'll bring the catch as early as we can. We should be able to sell it and get the boat cleaned before noon."

"Oh, thank you. I know she'll be happy." Elizabeth's face, too, was happy, and Adam's father gave her a thoughtful look.

7

Elizabeth was watching for Adam and his father the next morning, though they were earlier than she had expected. She helped Aunt Susan dress and eat breakfast while she thought they would be selling the fish. Then hastily she gathered up cleaning cloths and buckets and went running down to the harbor. The men were still bargaining, but they were lucky enough to have one merchant take the whole load.

By mid-morning the boat had been unloaded. Adam sloshed out the worst of the dirty water and fish scales, and Elizabeth scrubbed the rear of the boat where Aunt Susan would sit. She had made three trips back to the house for blankets and cushions, and now she was helping the older woman down the street.

It was a beautiful day, with the sun glittering on the little waves, and gulls soaring and cawing raucously overhead.

"Oh, I haven't been on a boat in years," said Aunt Susan. "I'd forgotten how much fun it is." She was trembling and shaking all over, but she smiled as she lifted her face to the breeze. "How far is it to Capernaum?" she asked.

"Well," Adam's father answered, "we don't have to go all the way there. Peter said last night that they are going to be walking along the coast today. He thought they might be by Magdala this afternoon."

And so it was. They could see the crowds of people even before they came into the little harbor, and when the men docked the ship, they could see one man especially, moving among the people.

As He came closer to the pier, the crowd pushed in till the ones in the boat could hardly see Him. Then as they watched, His friends seemed to make themselves a barrier around Him and pressed people back so only one could approach Him at a time.

Elizabeth sat there horrified as she saw the cripples so terribly bent and distorted, the blind reaching helplessly, men with running sores, and children flushed with fever or swollen and bloated with disease. Yet, one by one He touched and healed them.

At last she remembered what they had come for, and turned to Aunt Susan. Her eyes intent on the ones being healed. She seemed not even aware of Elizabeth or Adam or his father, there was such pity in her face.

Softly Elizabeth spoke. "Aunt Susan, let us go ashore now so that you can draw near."

Without turning her eyes from the healing even for a moment, she answered quietly, "No. No, I am not worthy." She took a deep breath. "What is my little trouble compared with so much pain?" But even as she spoke, such a light shone in her face that Elizabeth could not look away, and she heard the two men draw in a sudden breath.

And then it was over. Aunt Susan turned easily and spoke to Adam's father. "Thank you for bringing me. We will go home now, and perhaps you can be back in time for the night's fishing." She reached back and adjusted a cushion behind her.

"Aunt Susan!" Elizabeth exclaimed. "You are not shaking. You moved the cushion just where you wanted it!"

Aunt Susan looked startled. She lifted her hands and held them in front of her. They were still.

Adam and his father fell to their knees, but Aunt Susan cried out, "Don't kneel to me! Kneel to Him!" She reached for Elizabeth and hugged her close, then stood and raised her arms toward the sky. "O give thanks to the Lord for He is good, and his mercy endureth forever!"

It was a joyous trip back to Tiberias. Elizabeth could hardly wait to help Aunt Susan out of the boat to be sure she would walk easily on steady feet.

There she stood, straight and quiet, as she turned to Elizabeth. "Do you doubt?" she asked serenely. "I know I can walk. I could even run!"

As Susan stood happily on the pier, she reached smoothly into her basket and handed a roll of gold coins to Adam's father.

He took them hesitantly. "It is too much," he said humbly.

But she laughed with gladness. "Nothing is too much. May your daughters have fine husbands, and may your son be a blessing to your house!" Then she tucked her hand into Elizabeth's elbow, and they started up the street.

The next afternoon after Adam's father had sold their fish and he was sure Rachel's father had also returned to Capernaum, he walked up the village street to call on him. Ezra was in the courtyard resting under the tamarisk tree before he went back to mending his nets.

When he saw Adam's father approaching, he rose and greeted him courteously. "Rachel," he called as soon as they were seated, "bring a drink of cool water to our guest."

She appeared so immediately that Adam's father guessed she had just been waiting to be called. Well, that was as it should be. She brought first a basin of water and a towel to wash his feet and hands, kneeling quickly to perform this service, then hurried back into the house and brought cups of fresh water.

The men sat sipping the cool water and politely

asking about last night's catch, the possibilities for the next day's weather, the health of their families. At last Adam's father broached the subject he had come about, starting with praise of Rachel's courtesy and grace.

"Yes, she is a good girl," her father answered. "Each of my daughters will make some man a good wife."

Adam's father nodded. "It has long been my wish to have our families joined in marriage. My son has looked kindly on your daughter, and at last the time has come when we can discuss this seriously."

"It would indeed be an honor to our house to be joined with yours. I am sure my younger daughter will accept whatever plans I make on her behalf." Rachel's father spoke seriously, but he kept his eyes down lest his neighbor would see the glint in them. Adam's father had put off speaking for so long, let him take the leavings.

Unconcerned, Adam's father replied, "I am sure your younger daughter would accept whatever you arrange for her. However, as for me, I think your first daughter more appropriate for my son. We have been working hard, as you know, to pay for our new boat so that we could have greater income to provide for an increase in our family."

Rachel's father nodded. "You are to be congratulated on such a boat. What the family of Zabad makes is well built and will last for years." He expected the next comment to be an offer of certain boatloads of fish as a bride price, perhaps over a few months or even a year.

But Adam's father went on. "We realize the mar-riage of your capable elder daughter will be a loss to you and your wife. Therefore, we are happy to offer a recompense to you for a loss that will be our gain. We had expected to arrange for payment in kind, as our new boat is easy to handle and we bring in many fish. However, we have been fortunate and instead can offer you a bride price in gold." He brought out some of the coins Susan had given him the day before and held them in his hand.

Ezra's eyes snapped open, then lowered again to hide his thinking. Gold! That was different indeed. Even Nathan's uncle had offered only a camel, though of course it could be sold for a good price. Still it would have to be cared for until . . . Courtesy demanded that he make a response, but he wanted time to think this over.

"You are most generous toward my humble daughter. I shall indeed consider your suggestion favorably." Then he could not resist adding casually, "You may not have heard that I have been approached by a businessman of Jericho, and of course I had to consider my elder daughter first."

"And is she then betrothed?" asked the other man bluntly.

"Well, not formally," replied Ezra uneasily. The interview was not going quite as he had planned. "But as you know, my younger daughter—"

"Then if you wish to provide for your elder

daughter first," his neighbor interrupted, "I am pre-
pared to consider an immediate betrothal, once we
have settled the final details, of course."

He stood, and Ezra rose hurriedly also. "Time
enough, time enough," he protested. "Let us not be
hasty. I would need to send word to—to the other family, but the man involved is in Egypt, and I might not
get an answer for some little time."

"Well, I would be reasonable, of course, but my son
has waited patiently, and I feel that we should come to
a decision soon."

"Yes, yes," agreed Ezra, accompanying his guest to
the gate, "but in either case our families would be
united, an outcome I look forward to."

"I too look forward to the union, though I am not
sure it would be satisfactory 'in either case' as you say."

Adam's father took his leave and, with Ezra watching after him, walked away. As he remembered
Elizabeth in Tiberias, he thought the younger daughter
might be a good choice anyway, but he was not going
to let Ezra get the better of him—especially not with
gold in his hand. Besides, Adam had had his eye on
Rachel a long time, just like that ancient Jacob who
served seven years for his Rachel. Well, they would
just have to see. He meant to stand his ground. After
all, Adam was his only son.

8

IN THE DAYS AFTER THE MIRACLE, Aunt Susan
became more joyous at each new thing she found she
could do again. She could peel an orange! She could
eat without spilling her food; she could make bread
again without scattering the meal onto the floor. One
day she took out a shawl she had started to weave two
years earlier and found she could even hold the yarn
steady. At each new achievement, Elizabeth rejoiced
with her, but her heart sank when she was by herself.
She realized she would no longer be necessary here.
Yet there was no need for her at home, with Rachel still
there. Poor Rachel!

At last Aunt Susan noticed. "Elizabeth, why are
you no longer happy? You smile only when you think I
am watching. What has happened? Are you not happy
for me?"

"Oh, Aunt Susan, of course I am happy for you.

You have been so good to me. But now it is time I find other work. You no longer need me."

"No longer need you? Of course I need you. How can I enjoy my life if my only niece—" she reached out her arms, "—if my only niece, almost my daughter, is not with me?"

Elizabeth ran to her and knelt, but before she could say anything, Aunt Susan went on. "I have been thinking of traveling again as I did when my husband was alive, but a woman cannot do that alone. Will you go with me and be my help and companion?"

"Aunt Susan!" Elizabeth cried. "Do you mean it? Can I really stay with you? . . . and be a help?"

"A help!" exclaimed Aunt Susan. "You know my ways, and you can do so many things. And I will see things I haven't seen in years. And show them to you! My son will not need to worry that I am growing old before my time."

"But where would we go?" breathed Elizabeth. "What would we do?"

"Where would we go?" Aunt Susan asked, smiling at Elizabeth. "First we will go to my sister's home in Jericho. I have not seen her in two years. From there we will go into Jerusalem to give a thank offering in the temple. Then—oh, I don't know. Perhaps Caesarea. That's a beautiful city. Maybe we could even take a ship to Greece or go back down the coast to Egypt." She stretched her arms over her head. "I feel as if I were young again!"

At the names of such places, the thought of Nathan flashed into Elizabeth's mind. There had been no time when she had felt she could talk to Aunt Susan about him, and anyway what was the use? Nathan would not disgrace Rachel by withdrawing his offer, but even if he did, could Rachel's sister accept him? Her head drooped. She had been so sure when she had left him in the market, but really there was no way. Slowly she shook her head.

Then she thought again of Caesarea. If she must forget Nathan, at least she would be with Aunt Susan and see something of the world. Her lips began to curve and her eyes to sparkle.

"You will go!" exclaimed Aunt Susan. "You look happier already. Say you will stay with me. Say it!"

"I will, Aunt Susan. I will. I will." She scrambled to her feet. "When do we start? What shall I do first?"

Then a shadow crossed her face, and Susan, seeing it, asked, "What is it, child? What troubles you?"

"My family," answered Elizabeth. "My father must say whether I can go, and I would see my mother and Rachel before I leave. And Caleb," she added.

"But of course," agreed Aunt Susan. "When next your father comes to port, go home with him. You can tell him of our plans and talk with the others. I will send him a gold piece as surety that I will bring you back in time to be married."

"Married!" said Elizabeth with a laugh. "I am not even betrothed!"

"No, but you will be. I will see to that if he does not. Stay some days." Then she added hastily, "But not too long. I have need of you."

It was only two mornings later that Elizabeth saw her father's boat pulling into harbor. It was a humid day with promise of storm, so she knew he would be anxious to return as soon as he could. Quickly she packed a small bundle.

"Take cakes to Caleb," Aunt Susan reminded her, "and grapes and oranges to your mother and sister. And tie this carefully in your shawl so you will not lose it till you give it to your father." She placed a new gold coin in Elizabeth's hand. "Now be off and come safely back."

Her father looked worried when he saw her carrying a bundle, but she quickly called to him, "I come for a visit only, Father, and have need to talk with you when you are free." He nodded and went on with his business. She sat quietly on the bench where she had sat when she first came to Tiberias.

How much had changed since then! She counted back. Not quite four months, yet she had learned so much: how to shop in the big market, how to cook special foods, how to make the house more attractive, how to make Aunt Susan more comfortable.

And now Aunt Susan was well. How that changed everything! And Nathan—but she must not think about that.

Her father was motioning to her, so she picked up

her bundle and hurried to him. She had seen Adam and his father unloading their fish farther down the pier, but said nothing as she climbed into the boat. Her father quickly cast off the ropes. The clouds were getting darker, and the breeze was rising. She tied her shawl tighter to keep it from blowing off.

They were well toward Capernaum when the sudden blast of wind from the northwest hit them. Elizabeth's father struggled to lower the sail and keep the boat heading into the chopping waves. Elizabeth hung onto the rails as the boat pitched and rose and dived again. A huge wave broke over the side, drenching them both.

"Great God, help us," she whispered. She knew how quickly the storm could come up and had heard the men talking of its dreadful force. Now she could hardly see her father as the wind blew spume into her face, and waves washed up over the boat. She wished she could help bail out the water, but she was afraid to let go.

Suddenly a wilder blast tipped the boat on its side, and she saw her father thrown into the sea. Then the boat righted, with her still clinging to the rail, choking and half blinded. Frantically Elizabeth searched the waves. Where was her father? He could not swim, certainly, in such turmoil. As though that terrible wave had been the worst, the storm seemed to be subsiding, but the waves were still riotous.

Fearfully Elizabeth looked for a rope to throw out

to her father. Hand over hand, still holding the boat's edge, she got to the nearest rope and began loosening it. Where should she throw it? She searched the waves on the side where he had gone over, then turned to look back. There! Oh, thanks be to God!

She could see him clinging to a rope already. And then she saw the boat it was fastened to, dipping and lifting in the waves and spray. Adam's! Surely it was the new boat. She could see them now, pulling her father over the side. It was steadier than this one that was still rolling and tossing. Now they were coming nearer. They were close enough to throw a rope to her.

"Fasten it," she heard her father shout. But the rope slid back over the side before she could reach it. A second time. It missed entirely as the boat tipped away again. The third time Elizabeth grabbed it when it came over the side. She was thrown to her knees when the boat righted again, but she held onto the rope. For a minute she laughed helplessly, remembering how the camel had tipped her one way and then the other as it rose. But she hung on. Then the boat tilted, slackening the rope. Quickly she pulled it around a bar. It tightened, but she held on. The waves were easing, and a little at a time the other boat was lifting its sail. Jerkily she worked at pulling the rope another time around, and again, a little more each time it slackened.

"Hold it there!" Adam's father shouted. Elizabeth's fingers were clumsy and bleeding, but she managed to push the end through a loop so it pulled against itself.

She sat back on her heels and watched, ready to catch the end again if it loosened. It held. Slowly the other boat began to pull ahead, towing the one Elizabeth was in until they got to the stiller waters of the Capernaum harbor.

Men and women and children were gathered at the pier, for they had seen the boats in trouble and knew how dangerous the sudden storm could be. Elizabeth had sometimes stood there with them, before.

As soon as they had pulled the second boat near enough, Elizabeth's father jumped across into it and gathered her into his arms. "My daughter! Oh, I thought—"

Elizabeth's knees gave way, and she sagged against him. As if from a distance she could hear him saying, "My daughter. My daughter." And she whispered, "My father."

When at last the boat was secured, Elizabeth's mother, with Caleb sticking close, hurried them home. Rachel had run to the house as soon as she had seen the boats were safe and moved the simmering beans closer to the fire. She poured in more water and herbs to make a hot soup. Elizabeth and her father were soon out of their soaking clothes and into dry ones. Oh, how good it felt to be dry again. Elizabeth tried to sip the thin, hot broth, but her stomach was still in turmoil, and she set the cup down carefully.

When her father had finished his cup of soup and some bread, he started back to his boat. "I must see what damage was done," he said, when his wife tried to stop him. "And I have thinking to do."

At suppertime, he was very quiet. "No, the boat is not badly damaged. A day or two's mending will set things right. I've lost some nets, but they can be replaced." He bent to his meal.

After he had eaten, he left again without saying where he was going. When he returned, he sat down with them in the cool shadows of the courtyard.

"I could not rest," he said, "till I had made things right with Adam's father." Elizabeth heard Rachel draw in her breath sharply.

Her father went on. "I was angry when he came to ask for Rachel, but he did not remember that when I was in trouble." He paused, then continued. "It will be good to have our families joined, but only if it is a happy union for all. Therefore," he said, looking steadily at his wife, "two days from now we shall hold the betrothal feast. Rachel and Adam have served their families faithfully. They shall now be betrothed, and married as soon as seems wise."

Rachel ran to her father and knelt, but had no words as he placed his hands on her head and gave her his blessing.

The next day Elizabeth could hardly believe the change in Rachel. She was as she had been in the days when they were children. She sang under her breath the rejoicing psalms of David. She teased Caleb and played with him. She ran to help where there was need instead of just plodding through the day. She smiled!

The betrothal day was beautiful, sunny and cool, with just a hint of breeze. Adam's family came at mid-morning, along with the village elders who had been invited to witness the betrothal. Elizabeth was delighted to be there. If she had been in Tiberias, she would not even have known till after the ceremony!

Their mother and the girls had been busy all the day before. Clothes had been washed and aired. The house was scrubbed and freshened with herbs. Piles of bread and cakes had been baked, and dates, oranges, and grapes had been brought from the market. Now the smell of roasting lamb promised a real feast.

Dressed in their best, Rachel and Adam stood before their families—and before all the world as far as they were concerned—to make their betrothal covenant. Adam had brought a parchment written by a scribe to give to his bride's father. There were other gifts, but they would be presented later when the festivities began.

Now he stood beside Rachel to give the age-old promise. The group was silent as he spoke directly to her. "According to the ancient customs of our people, I spread the corner of my garment over you." Solemnly he lifted the edge of his loose outer cloak and enclosed Rachel in it. She glanced up at him and down again, blushing, as he continued formally. "On this day I give my solemn oath and covenant that you are now my wife and I your husband."

At the last word the friends and family shouted in joy and crowded around the couple to wish them all blessings and honor.

That evening after the guests had left, Elizabeth suddenly remembered the gold she had been given for her father. "My shawl!" she exclaimed. "Did I still have it on after the storm? Where is it?"

"I washed it with the other things," her mother replied calmly, "and put what was tied in it under a stone in the hearth. Come."

They went into the house, and Elizabeth breathed a sigh of relief as she took the gold piece and hurried back out to her father.

She sat by him and said, "You remember I said I had to talk with you. There has been so much excitement we had no time. Now I will tell you what Aunt Susan plans and why I came for a visit and not to stay."

"You would be welcome, my daughter," her father answered in a softer voice than she had heard him use in some time.

"I thank you," she said, smiling at him and then at her mother, "but I have a story to tell."

She felt Caleb cuddle comfortably beside her.

Starting with her asking Adam and his father to take Aunt Susan in their boat, she told of the rabbi she had seen again, of the wretched people who had come for help, and of the many healings He had performed. She told of watching from the boat, and then, breathlessly, of the miracle for Aunt Susan.

9

"AND NOW THAT SHE IS WELL and able to move again," Elizabeth went on, "she wants to go to Jericho and Jerusalem, and perhaps to Caesarea and beyond. And she wants me to go with her, because a woman alone cannot travel so."

Her father nodded slowly. "And when would you come back?" he asked.

"That I know not," she answered. "Perhaps in a month or two, perhaps a year. In the meantime she sent you this gold coin as surety that she would bring me back, and that you would someday have a bride price for me."

She hesitated as he took it. Should she ask about Nathan? He would be free now. Or perhaps not. Perhaps somewhere in Egypt—perhaps he would not come back at all, or would come back betrothed to someone else. She remained silent.

Her father was slowly turning the coin in his fingers. Then he looked up and smiled at her. "When that day comes," he said, "I will have this strung on a chain of gold for the bride to wear. Go with my blessing and come back in safety."

He rose and kissed her on each cheek and went into the house. It was time for Caleb, too, to go to bed, so they soon left the starlit courtyard and settled happily for the night.

Elizabeth stayed at home three days more, doing what she could to help her mother, playing with Caleb, talking with Rachel, and feeling closer to her father than she ever had before. At last, however, she said good-bye and left with her father when he took his fish to Tiberias.

She had much to tell Aunt Susan after the first greetings and excitement: the terrible storm, the rescue, Rachel's betrothal. Aunt Susan was delighted that she was back and had much to tell her, too. She had ordered a new robe for herself and one for Elizabeth, as well as new shawls. She had sent word to her sister that they would be coming in a week or two. Her son was enquiring about a caravan they could join and had hired two donkeys for them to ride.

"But I can walk," Elizabeth protested.

"I, too, now," agreed Aunt Susan proudly, "but we're not going to! I will not run the risk of appearing footsore and weary when I have sent word that I am well. Imagine my sister's face when she hears the whole story! I can scarcely wait to tell her."

They hardly stopped talking the whole afternoon, but after supper Aunt Susan became so quiet that Elizabeth wondered if something were wrong after all. She thought back over the day but could think of nothing that should have been troubling.

At last she asked directly, "Is something wrong, Aunt Susan?"

She glanced at Elizabeth quickly, then shook her head. "Not wrong, but I just don't quite know how to say this. I cannot talk with your mother, and I don't want to send someone to talk with your father for fear—" She broke off and sat pleating the cloth over her knees. After a minute she began again. "Come sit by me, child, so I can see your face and know if I offend you."

Elizabeth came without hesitation and dropped to the floor by Aunt Susan. "You know you can't offend me," she said. "You have been so good to me."

Aunt Susan smiled shortly then her face sobered as she began. "You have seen my son almost daily when he has brought things from the market. And he has seen you. You may not know that his wife and baby died in childbirth only a year after they were married. Since then he has seen no one he has thought to make his wife."

Elizabeth lowered her head, for she could not bear the sadness in the face above her. In the pit of her stomach, she had a feeling what was going to be asked.

Aunt Susan went on. "While you were away, he talked with me. Jonah knows he is much older than you, and he would wait. He thought if you were—were not opposed, he would talk with your father. Perhaps he has other plans for you. But if not, and if you were willing, perhaps you could be betrothed before we left, or when we came back if you wanted more time. Jonah is a kind man, and he would make you a good husband."

"I know he is," whispered Elizabeth. "I am sure he would, but . . ." She sat silently, not knowing how to go on.

"Does that mean no?" Aunt Susan asked quietly. "Or just that you had not even thought about it? Oh, my dear, I'd love to have you for a daughter!"

"And I to be a daughter to you," Elizabeth replied warmly. "But he has been hurt before, and I would not want to be the one to hurt him again. I do not—love him."

"Do not—or cannot?" asked Aunt Susan softly. "Our people have a saying, 'Love comes after marriage.' "

Elizabeth nodded. "That's what my mother says, but it is not always so. With Rachel, love came first."

"And with you?" asked Aunt Susan, putting her hand under Elizabeth's chin and lifting her face. "Is there someone already?"

"There might be," Elizabeth whispered, closing her eyes as a blush burned up into her face.

The older woman sighed as she looked at her. "Yes,

there might be. Can you trust me enough to tell me about him?"

"I would trust you with anything," Elizabeth answered softly, opening her eyes. She drew a deep breath. "It happened before I came here, but then there was a time after, too."

Slowly she settled back onto a cushion and began telling Aunt Susan of Caleb's going with the camel train, of her chase to catch up with him, and of the man who had left his caravan to bring her and her little brother safely home.

When she stopped, Aunt Susan waited a few minutes, then gently prompted her. "You said there was one time since you came here. I have not seen him?"

Elizabeth shook her head. "He was in the market-place." She told of the surprise of meeting him, and his telling of having sent a messenger to her father. She told of his anger and disappointment when he found he had offered marriage with the wrong daughter.

"Oh, Aunt Susan, he said he wanted to marry me. I know he should not have talked to me, but he did. And now Rachel is betrothed, and he is free, though he does not know it. He wanted to marry me, but he would not bring shame on Rachel by withdrawing. And he is kind, too, and considerate. He would be a good father, as he was to Caleb that night, and—and—we laugh at the same things—and he said he would come back, and I said I would not get tired of waiting."

Aunt Susan was smiling. "Did you think of all

those reasons why he would be a good husband, or did you just look at him and he at you, and you were sure?"

"Oh, Aunt Susan," exclaimed Elizabeth, "how did you know?"

The older woman reached out and gently smoothed Elizabeth's hair. "Because, child, that is the way it happened to me."

Elizabeth lifted a radiant face. "It was? It truly was?"

"It truly was. But, oh, my child, if he does not come back, will you remember my son? I will tell him it cannot be now, perhaps never, but I know he will not easily turn his face to another."

The look of sadness swept over her face again, but she banished it with a smile. "And now we must go to bed. It has been a beautiful day, but strenuous, and there will be another tomorrow."

It was, after all, ten days before they started for Jericho. At first Elizabeth had tried to be busy in another part of the house whenever Aunt Susan's son brought fish or fruit from the market. However, he was no different than he had been before, so she was again at ease.

The morning they were to join the caravan, he was there early with the donkeys and helped fasten their bundles onto the saddles. "Take my greetings to the House of Judah," he reminded his mother, "and may the Lord keep you safe till you return." He kissed her on both cheeks, than helped her onto the donkey.

Elizabeth was startled by the name Judah, but she tried not to show she had heard what they had said. Easily she jumped onto her donkey and settled herself before Jonah turned to her. "I thank you for going with my mother," he said formally, his hand on the donkey's bridle. "You are like a daughter to her, and I let her go more confidently, knowing you are with her." He looked at her steadily and added, "May you come back safely for us all."

Elizabeth dropped her eyes as he let go of the reins and stepped back. "Thank you for your trust," she said in a low voice. "I shall try to be worthy."

The sounds of the last "God bless and keep you" chimed together as they started along the street to meet the pack train of donkeys carrying wool to Jerusalem.

Before mid-morning they had reached the southern end of the Sea of Galilee and started toward the highlands of Samaria. On the Passover trips Elizabeth's family had crossed the Jordan to go south, so she had not come this way before. She watched the countryside in delight. In the spring, the almond trees had been in rosy bloom, and hyacinths and cyclamen had dotted the way. Now it was summer. By small villages there were many gardens, and in bigger fields grain was ripening. Laurel was blooming along hidden waterways, and trees were in full leaf. Several times she saw flocks of sheep in the distance gathered in the shade of a big oak or tamarisk tree. Even the vultures hovering in the distance lifted her heart with their freedom and power.

Elizabeth looked for places she had come by when she had brought Caleb back, but the well was all she really recognized.

Before they got to Jericho, there were more barren areas, mountains of rock and sand with not a tree, and dry wadis where water had run after the winter rains. But how different when they came in sight of Jericho, with its palm trees, orange trees, and big sycamores! Houses were surrounded by gardens filled with flowers and vegetables, and now and then she caught the sound of running water.

The last night, they had stayed at the caravansary at El Bireh, and that night Elizabeth finally asked Aunt Susan about the family where they were to visit. "I hope you did not think I was listening, but I heard your son send greetings to the House of Judah. Is that where we are going in Jericho?" She hesitated. "Is—is it a big family? Or are there many families of that name? It is an ancient name, of course."

"Yes, but I really don't know much about the family. It is my sister, you see, and though I've often been there to visit, I don't know much about all her husband's family. I know he has two brothers, but I don't know where they live, even. Hannah is my older sister, and she and her husband had six boys but no girls."

She smiled at Elizabeth. "That's why you are my

only niece. But nephews . . . There are Eliab and Dan—he's the same age as my son—and Benjamin and Josiah and Eli. They're all married and have children of their own, except the youngest, Nathan. . . ."

Elizabeth's heart began to pound. Nathan bar Judah. Could it be? It must be!

10

ELIZABETH CLASPED HER HANDS tightly and began
to listen again. Aunt Susan was going on. ". . . in his
twenties and should be married, but he wasn't even
betrothed the last I heard." She paused and then said
as if to herself, "And I had only one child. Hannah is
so rich in children." Then she brightened. "Well, we
take what the Lord sends, and I am grateful for the
one. Now let us sleep, for you will have many new
people to meet tomorrow."

Elizabeth nodded. She didn't dare ask any more,
but it was long before she got to sleep.

The welcome at Jericho was a joyous one, with
everybody talking at once, then cool water to wash
away the dust of travel, and bundles to be opened
with Aunt Susan's gifts to everyone.

Over and over she told of the miracle that had
healed her. She described the rabbi and the crowds

that had come for His help. "Especially the children," she said, her face reflecting her grief at the terrible diseases, but also the excitement as first one and then another had been made whole.

"And tomorrow I shall go to the temple in Jerusalem. I shall give a thank offering for the Lord's gift to me through this rabbi." She held up her hands. "Oh, Hannah, you can't know what it was like to be shaking so. I could not eat without spilling food like a baby. I could not comb my hair decently till this one came." She smiled and slid her arm around Elizabeth's shoulders.

"Wait until you are rested to go," urged Hannah.

"No. Tomorrow. I have waited long enough. Surely I must send a sweet savor to the Lord."

"Then I shall send word to my sons and their families. You must see them, and how my grandchildren have grown." She counted on her fingers. "Tomorrow you go to Jerusalem. The sabbath begins at sundown the next day and lasts till sundown the day after. But the fourth day we will have a family supper. You will have made your offering and be at peace, and I shall have had time to prepare special things that they like. Oh, Susan," Hannah cried, hugging her, "I am so glad you came!"

Before dawn the next morning Elizabeth and Aunt Susan were on their way to Jerusalem. It would be a long day, but their sturdy little donkeys would get them home by dark.

As they approached the city, they could see the golden rim of the Temple gleaming in the sunlight. The higher they climbed toward it, the more crowded the streets became. Elizabeth pulled her shawl carefully around her, the way Aunt Susan had, while she watched the activity about them. There was a man with a strip of leather over his shoulder to show he was a tanner, and another man was carrying pigeons for sale.

She remembered walking up the hill as a child with her family and being jostled and crowded because she was so small. Now she smiled happily as she looked around, able to see over people's heads to the narrow shops. Some had jewelry displayed in the window, and others had baskets of fresh fruit half filling the doorway.

Outside the temple they dismounted, and Aunt Susan gave a little boy a coin to hold their donkeys. Pushing along with the crowd, they entered the Court of the Gentiles. There Elizabeth waited while Aunt Susan changed her Galilean coins for the temple coins required for the offering, and then they went on into the Court of the Women.

Elizabeth remembered wondering as a child why it was called the Court of the Women when there were so many men there, too, but her mother had explained that it was as far into the temple as women could go.

Now she walked quietly beside Aunt Susan as she went to the trumpet-shaped chest where thank offerings were given. As Aunt Susan dropped her generous handful of coins, Elizabeth looked again in awe at the golden vine along one wall.

In a brisk voice Aunt Susan interrupted her dreaming. "Now let us climb the steps and look over the wall. It has been so long since I have seen the altar of sacrifice."

Elizabeth smiled as she remembered the last time she had come. "I'm tall enough to see over, but Mother had to lift Caleb up the last time we were here."

They climbed the steps to the great Nicanor Gate, then walked along the gallery where other women were standing. They stood quietly a few minutes, watching the priests at the huge stone altar. Softly Aunt Susan said, "Great and beautiful are the gold and marble we have seen. But how much, much greater is the one God whom we cannot see!"

Elizabeth nodded humbly, and they turned to go back down the steps, through the courts, and out of the mighty temple.

The next day the household was full of bustle with the women preparing for the sabbath, but at sundown, peace settled over the household. And on the sabbath, Elizabeth had time not only to go to the synagogue with the family, but to rest and think of her family, and the changes a few months had brought.

The day after the sabbath, Elizabeth was up early and went out into the garden almost before dawn. She was wandering along the paths, touching a flower here, or stopping to listen to a bird's waking song, when she heard steps behind her.

She turned and saw Hannah coming toward her. "You are up early, child," she said as she approached.

Elizabeth nodded. "You have such a beautiful garden. We have gardens at home, but not so lush and plentiful as this."

"Isn't it strange," agreed Hannah softly, "that the Lord should put this beautiful oasis in the midst of such barrenness? Like parts of our lives. But tell me about Galilee. I have never been there, but my son tells me that it is beautiful, too."

"In a different way," Elizabeth said thoughtfully. "It is green or gold, also, but spread out more. There is room for flocks of sheep and for fields of grain." She smiled, thinking of the two places. "Galilee is like a platter while Jericho is a cup."

"And the Sea of Galilee?" the other woman asked.

"That is so different, it is hard to say. Sometimes it has terrible storms." She shivered as she remembered the one she had been in. "Other days it is calm and peaceful. It reflects the mountains from the other side. I liked to see it that way when I worked at drying fish, and I liked to hear gulls crying as they came soaring and diving in."

Hannah looked at her questioningly. "You worked at drying fish? Is your father a fisherman, then?"

"Yes, though I did not work with him. He sold his fish there in Capernaum or in Tiberias. That is how I came to work for Aunt Susan." She blushed and explained, "Of course you know she is not really my aunt, but she has been so good to me."

One of the maids hurried up behind them with a message for her mistress. As she started to turn away, Elizabeth asked, "Is there something I can do to help? I would be glad to."

Hannah smiled but shook her head. "Enjoy the garden, and come in for bread when you will. I think Susan is still sleeping." She went back to the house, talking quietly with the maid.

At first Elizabeth felt out of place when the family began to arrive, but everybody was friendly, and for a while Aunt Susan kept her close. Everybody there wanted to hear about the miracle, and they wondered whether that rabbi would ever come to Jericho. "Maybe Jerusalem, anyway," someone suggested. "That would be near enough so we could go to see and hear Him."

There were so many of the family that instead of using a table Hannah loaded big trays with the roasted lamb and bread and olives and cheese. These she set in the courtyard, where the men and older boys could gather round them. Later the maids brought other trays heaped with grapes and oranges and fresh figs. When those were finished, the women and younger children gathered around the trays inside, leaving the men to talk business by themselves.

After they had eaten, the two littlest grandchildren

were put to bed for their naps. Then Elizabeth asked, "Who wants a story?"

"Me!"

"Me, too!" the others shouted, so she gathered them around her in the far corner of the room.

"What story shall I tell?"

"Joseph in Egypt," called out one. "That's where Uncle Nathan is now."

Then another shouted out, "Moses and the burning bush." One of the little boys, who made her think of Caleb, snuggled close and whispered. "All about Moses. Start when he was a baby in a basket."

She smiled and cuddled him closer. "That's a good idea," she said. "Then it will be about Egypt, too." Glad that she could be of some use, she started the story, too busy watching the children's faces to notice the glances that passed among the women or hear what they talked about. . . .

"If only Nathan could have been here," his mother said with a sigh, "all my boys would have been together." But she soon brightened. "Jeremiah—that's my husband's brother—" she reminded Susan, "Jeremiah says Nathan will soon be back. He sent Nathan to Egypt on business, you know," she added proudly.

"Are plans made yet for his wedding?" Susan asked. "He's the last one of your boys to be married. Surely he should be settling down?"

Hannah nodded. "Soon. Soon, I'm sure. Jeremiah talked with us about a family in Galilee, in Capernaum,

I believe, but he sent Nathan off before the plans could be settled. Surely when he gets back there will be a betrothal," she added, smiling confidently. "I haven't seen the girl, of course, but Jeremiah said it is a respected family, and Nathan was very eager."

Susan almost held her breath, remembering Elizabeth's story. Why in the world had she not asked the young man's name? Did Elizabeth even know it? Or was that why she had asked about the House of Judah? She kept her head down so nobody would see her excitement. "Do you know the family name?" she asked quietly.

"The father is a fisherman, Ezra bar Laban, I think Jeremiah said. I suppose there was haggling over the bride price, and Jeremiah's business in Egypt wouldn't wait."

She glanced quickly at the corner where the children were listening intently. "I wish the girl were somebody like your Elizabeth, Susan," she went on. "If the other doesn't work out, I'll give Jeremiah a hint. Or is she promised already?"

Susan shook her head and answered only, "She will be a good wife. Your Nathan could not do better." Hearing the father's name, she was sure, but she would say nothing further till she could talk to Hannah alone. *If it can't be my son,* she thought, *at least it can be my nephew.*

The days slipped by fast, with visiting, shopping in the markets, and all the daily tasks. Susan wanted to talk to her sister about Elizabeth, but each day she put it off, hoping that Nathan might return so there would be no possible mistake.

At last she could wait no longer, for they planned to leave for Caesarea with the next caravan to the coast, and that might be any day. The two women were sitting in the courtyard alone, while Elizabeth had gone with one of the maids to get water from the well.

"Hannah," Susan began, "I have something to tell you. It is not my story alone, so I have put off talking with you, but there is a message I think you should give Nathan when he gets home, or perhaps tell Jeremiah."

She had tried to plan how she would tell the story so that Elizabeth might never be embarrassed if Hannah did become her mother-in-law. Hannah did love to talk, and there were neighbors to be considered. Now Hannah was waiting, and yet she hesitated.

11

At last Susan began, "You said when I first came that you wished Nathan's wife might be like Elizabeth. Well, she may be Elizabeth."

Hannah looked up sharply. "May be Elizabeth?" she repeated. "What do you mean?"

"I did not tell you before," Susan explained, "because it was not my story to tell, and I was hoping Nathan would return before we left, but I'm sure she is the one Nathan wanted. Her father is Ezra bar Laban of Capernaum."

Hannah's face broke into a smile. "You don't say so! Then why the delay? Did she know? Surely Jeremiah would not deny a fair bride price. And it is time Nathan was married. I want to live long enough to see his children."

Carefully Susan went on. "There was a misunderstanding, I believe. Many fathers want to have their elder daughter married first. But anyway, the other daughter is now betrothed, so that is settled."

"Oh, Susan," Hannah interrupted, "don't raise my hopes if it cannot be. I want to see Nathan married and hold his first son in my arms. You're sure she is not promised elsewhere?"

Susan's face saddened. "I think she—could be, but I do not think she is." Her hands tightened in her lap. "If Jeremiah were to talk with the family now, the problem could be settled. Or when Nathan comes back, if all are satisfied, perhaps he could go himself."

"But she would not be there if she goes with you," Hannah objected. "If her father agreed, of course, there could be the official betrothal, but I think Nathan would not be satisfied till he had seen her." She glanced toward the door, hearing the girls' voices and laughter as they came from the well.

"True," Susan agreed. "I have thought about that. We are going to Joppa and then to Caesarea. I want Elizabeth to see something of the world. We will stay some time at the home of Samuel bar David in Caesarea, whose wife is my friend of long standing. I had thought to go on from there, but the season is passing so swiftly I think we might come back to Tiberias for the winter. It is not a good time to be traveling then. And there he would find us easily."

She stopped as Elizabeth came in the door laughing. "You should have seen the girls try to ride a camel! There was a man in the street who offered them a ride in return for their drawing water, but he didn't warn them the way Nathan did me—" She clapped her hand over her mouth.

Hannah jumped up. "Is Nathan home? Have you seen him?"

Elizabeth shook her head and looked pleadingly at Aunt Susan, who smiled at her serenely. "I have told Hannah that your father is Ezra bar Laban, and that Nathan bar Judah's uncle had talked with him about marriage."

Elizabeth sank to her knees before Hannah. "I would not have you think—" she began.

But Hannah took her hands and raised her to her feet. "Do not kneel, child. I could not be happier than to have you betrothed to my son."

"But I am not," Elizabeth protested in a whisper.

"But you would not object?" the older woman asked.

Elizabeth lifted her head with shining eyes. "Object? How could I object?" Then she bowed her head again. "But he may not want—perhaps in Egypt—or his uncle may have arranged—" She stumbled into silence.

Hannah laughed softly. "We will let those worries take care of themselves. I know my son. Come now and sit with us. Tell me, when Nathan returns, have you a message for him?"

Elizabeth's mind was in turmoil. A message? What could she say that would not sound bold and forward? That would still leave him free if he no longer cared?

At last she spoke quietly. "Just tell him Rachel, my sister, is betrothed to Adam."

"That is all?"

"That is all," she repeated.

Hannah could not sit quietly. She was more excited than Elizabeth as she jumped to her feet and paced back and forth across the floor. Clasping and unclasping her hands, she said at last, "Surely I can tell him—" She paused, looking thoughtfully at the girl before her.

Elizabeth's throat was tight, but she answered quietly, "You are his mother and can tell him what you will. If you do not think me suitable . . . But I cannot tell him more. It is for him to decide if anything else is to be said."

The next morning they left early on the road to Joppa. They were to spend one night on the way and then stay for some days at the home of a friend of Aunt Susan's. Then they would go on up the coast road to Caesarea.

This part of the country Elizabeth had never seen. Crossing the hills was not so different from other parts of Judea, but when they started down the other side and came in sight of the Great Sea, she was breathless. The closer they got the bigger it seemed. The water went on and on to the horizon. She thought of the Sea of Galilee, but it was only a pool compared with this sea she had heard called the Mediterranean. At Capernaum the hills across the water had been blue against the sky, but here there were no hills beyond, just waves rolling and tumbling as far as she could see.

The first morning in Joppa she went out early to look again at this great sea of water. It was a windy morning. The horizon was gray with waves running and breaking white at their tops. Elizabeth was reminded of the storm she had been in on Galilee. But here the waves seemed to stop in a long, white line.

Behind her the family's only daughter, Dorcas, came running down the path. She was younger than Elizabeth, but excited to have company. "Good morning," she sang out.

Elizabeth turned a puzzled face to her. She returned Dorcas's greeting and then asked, "Why do the waves stop out there? It looks like a storm, but it's quiet here in the harbor."

Dorcas nodded. "My father says there's a reef out there, a whole line of rocks under the water. They stop the big waves and keep the boats safe once they're in the harbor. Don't you have reefs in Galilee?"

Elizabeth shook her head. "I don't think so. When we have a storm, the wind drives the waves all over. I was in a storm not long ago." She told Dorcas about it as they scrambled down closer to the water.

When they got to the edge, Dorcas went on, "Joppa is a very old harbor. Some people even say Noah's ark was here."

"Really?" asked Elizabeth, as she stood staring out toward the horizon again. "But where is Greece?" she asked, frowning thoughtfully. "I thought it was across the sea this way."

Dorcas smiled, proud to be able to tell this stranger so many things. "Oh, it is," she said. "My father sails there to trade for pottery and other things. But it's a long ways. Sometimes he's away for weeks. When he comes back, though, he always brings me something. See? This little ring is what he brought me last time."

That was the beginning of an enchanted time for Elizabeth. Morning after morning she hurried down to the harbor to watch the water break over the reef. Later in the day the two girls explored the markets with Aunt Susan and Dorcas's mother. "Look!" Dorcas would point out. "My father brings these dishes from Greece. See their design?" Sometimes a shopkeeper greeted her especially because he knew her father. Others even treated her and Elizabeth to candied almonds or little cakes fresh from the oven at coffee time.

On the day they were leaving for Caesarea, Elizabeth could hardly bear to say good-bye. When would she and Dorcas see each other again? She drew Aunt Susan aside and whispered to her, "Would you mind if I gave Dorcas the shawl you bought for me in Tiberias? I would like to give her something."

"Of course I would not mind, child," Aunt Susan answered. "I should have thought to give you money to buy a gift for her."

Elizabeth shook her head. "I would rather give her something of mine."

But before she could give it to her, Dorcas had slipped from her own finger the little gold ring she had showed Elizabeth the first day. "Wear it for me," she said, taking Elizabeth's hand. "We'll be friends as long as you wear it."

Elizabeth hugged her. "That will be till we're old, old ladies," she said. Then she draped her own lacy blue shawl over Dorcas's head.

"Now I am a grown-up lady," said Dorcas, laughing. They kissed each other on both cheeks and ran happily to the waiting donkeys.

If Joppa had been exciting, Elizabeth thought, Caesarea would be even more so. Aunt Susan had told her about King Herod's building the magnificent hippodrome and the aqueducts—things she had never heard of before—and rich people from all over the country were moving there for business and building lovely homes.

Aunt Susan's friends whom they were visiting had just finished building a new house in Roman style. It was beautiful, and it even had a pool in the main reception room—they called it an atrium—and pillars lining the halls on each side. So many rooms seemed to open off the halls on each side, Elizabeth hoped she would not walk into the wrong one by mistake.

She was supposed to sleep in the room next to Aunt Susan's. "Can't I bring my blanket in and sleep on the floor by you?" she asked.

Aunt Susan smiled and gave her hand a squeeze,

but shook her head. "It would be discourteous not to do as they have planned," she whispered.

Elizabeth blushed, for she didn't want to be rude, certainly not to Aunt Susan's friends. It was not cozy, though, like home where they all slept in one room.

The first morning when she woke up, Elizabeth hurried out, thinking she could see the garden, but there wasn't one. She wandered around the big court-yard, looking at the marble statues and the tubs of flowers here and there. The statues bothered her. Didn't the Lord say they were to make no graven images?

She looked over the courtyard wall and down toward the harbor. Already there were men hurrying around, loading and unloading the big ships. Some of these ships were even bigger than the ones at Joppa. "Oh, if we were only going on board today," she murmured.

"Are you not, then, happy with us?" asked a man's voice behind her.

Elizabeth whirled around. It was their host, the husband of Aunt Susan's friend. "Oh," she gasped, "of course I'm happy here. You have a beautiful home. I was just thinking how exciting it would be to sail to—to Athens, or Alexandria, or someplace like that."

"Have you ever been on a ship?" he asked.

"Not a big one. My father is a fisherman on the Sea of Galilee, and I've been on his boat."

"Would you like to come down with me this morning? I have business near the harbor."

"Oh, may I? Can we really go onto a ship?"

The man clapped his hands once, and a maid came running. "Come with us to the harbor," he said. "I am going to take our guest aboard a ship, and then you can come back with her."

It was an exciting morning. The ship they went on was so big it had an extra sail above the main one, as well as oars for a dozen men on each side. The upper sail was even embroidered with purple thread. The deck where they walked was inlaid with ivory. Below it was a big hold, where men were storing jars of wine and oil, and a small section for passengers. When her host finally took her back onto the wharf, Elizabeth thanked him, her whole face glowing.

"You enjoyed it?" he asked. "My daughter Miriam doesn't like to come down with me."

"It was wonderful," she exclaimed. "How could she not like it?" Then she blushed at seeming critical. "But of course she has seen more than I have. There are so many things in the world I've never seen—"

"And the world is bigger than Judea," he finished, smiling down at her.

She nodded, but before she could say anything more, he went on. "My wife and daughter will take you to the markets, I'm sure, with all their exotic goods, but someday would you like to see ordinary, practical things like the aqueduct to bring water into the city?"

"Ordinary things!" she exclaimed. "That's not

ordinary. At home we go to the well and bring water home in jars."

He laughed and said, "You're right. We really don't think it's ordinary either, but we like to pretend we're used to such things. Now the maid will stay with you as you go back through the streets, and we'll see what else we can plan."

12

For Elizabeth, each day brought something new. On the sabbath they went to the synagogue, which was twice as big as the one in Capernaum. The rabbis with beautiful voices intoned the Scripture. Yet as she listened, Elizabeth thought back to the One who had spoken so simply, but with authority—and healing power. She wondered if He would heal Uncle Levi's blindness if they went to Him when she got back.

One afternoon Miriam came to Elizabeth's room. "Mother suggested I help with your cosmetics," she said with a smile. She gestured to the maid following her with a tray of little bottles and boxes.

"Oh, no, thank you," protested Elizabeth. "I don't wear any of those things."

"Now is the time to start, then," said the older girl. "I had an Egyptian maid before this one, and she taught me. It's fun, really. I'll show you how."

Elizabeth was about to object again when Miriam added, "Mother is having other guests this evening, and she thought you might like to look more—modern."

Elizabeth blushed. She didn't want Aunt Susan's friend to be ashamed of her looks.

Miriam had taken the tray from the maid and put it on a table near the window. "Come sit where the light is good," she invited. Hesitantly, Elizabeth did as she was told, and Miriam tipped her face, looking at her from this angle and that.

Suddenly she smiled. "You really have a beautifully shaped face," she said. "Just wait till I get some more color in it." She turned to the tray and picked up a little alabaster box. "When you're all done, I'll let you look in my bronze mirror," she said, "but now don't even try to guess what I'm doing."

She touched her finger to the paste in the box and rubbed it gently onto Elizabeth's cheeks. "Someday I'll show you what I use, and you can try it yourself," she murmured as she concentrated on what she was doing.

Her fingers were so gentle Elizabeth began to relax. Miriam used a cream and a powder and a soft little brush all over Elizabeth's face. "Now your eyes," she said, taking a little blue stick from the tray. "Look up so I can draw a line on your lower lid. Good. Now down, till I do the upper lids. That's it."

She stepped back and clapped her hands as Elizabeth opened her eyes. "Oh, they look ever so much larger. Now, I'll darken your eyelashes. There. Look."

She handed Elizabeth the little bronze mirror. Elizabeth could not believe the elegant face looking back at her, and Miriam laughed. "Not the same girl at all, are you?" she asked. "Wait till my brother sees you."

She laid the last things back on the tray. "I'll leave my maid to do your hair while I go make up my face, and we'll be sisters tonight. I'll come get you when it's time."

"Oh, I can comb—"

"No, Tessa knows how to do it with a few curls, and here's a narrow, gold turban. She'll wind it on for you." And she was gone.

After the maid had finished, Elizabeth sat stiffly by the window. She felt as if she should not move for fear her hair would fall down or her face would crack. She wished she could talk with Aunt Susan, but she didn't dare go to her room for fear Miriam would come and not find her.

When she did come, she exclaimed, "Oh, lovely. I was sure Tessa could do it. Come now." She slipped her arm through Elizabeth's and led her proudly into the reception room.

To Elizabeth it looked full of strangers, though there were really only three other families. Her eyes searched fearfully for Aunt Susan, and when she saw her smile, she felt more easy. Aunt Susan never used all those things on her face, and Elizabeth had been afraid she would be shocked.

As she began to relax and look around, she saw

how many tables were set in the courtyard. Were the women going to eat with the men? She could feel herself blushing at the thought. She hadn't minded when it was just Miriam's father, but . . .

Before she really had time to worry, Miriam's mother came to her with a smile. "How beautiful you look tonight," she said. "Miriam, be sure you introduce Elizabeth to everybody. Here is my son, Asher, for a start. He is just back from Jerusalem."

Elizabeth looked up at the handsome young man beside her, but her eyes fell before the blaze in his. His voice was casual, though, as he asked courteously, "Have you visited in Jerusalem?"

"Oh, yes," she replied, relieved that they had something in common to talk about. "The temple is magnificent. My family and I have been there almost every year for Passover." As she thought of the gold and marble, she forgot about her face, and her usual happiness shone through the makeup. "And I just went there about a month ago with Aunt Susan."

"What do you think of Caesarea in comparison?" he asked. "Of course, we don't have the temple, but we do have other attractions."

"You can brag about Caesarea later," interrupted his sister, laughing. "I have to introduce Elizabeth to the others, and it's nearly time for dinner to be served. I'm famished."

In a daze, Elizabeth walked around with Miriam. She tried to remember the names and faces. She wanted to visit with people, but everybody was moving and chattering. They would hardly get started talking when someone else would interrupt.

In Joppa, Dorcas had shown her how to recline at the table, so she could do that easily, but she had expected to be by Aunt Susan. Instead, Miriam kept Elizabeth by her, with Asher on the other side. Every now and then he gave her a special tidbit, an extra large grape, or a piece of honey cake, but there didn't seem much chance to talk. Everybody was calling out to him, asking about his trip to Jerusalem or telling him of the latest races in the hippodrome or the most recent cargo from Egypt.

When Elizabeth was finally back in her room, she felt exhausted. There was so much to think about, and she suddenly remembered she had not asked Miriam how to take off the cosmetics. Did she just wash her face as usual?

While she was puzzling over that, Miriam slipped in. "I just thought—I didn't leave you any oil to take the colors off with." She had a small bottle in her hand. "Let me show you." She took out the glass stopper and tipped some onto her finger. After dabbing it around Elizabeth's eyes and on her cheeks, she wiped it off with a soft cloth. "Now you can wash your face. Then put just a little of this cream on for the night." She smiled and turned to the door. "Sleep well," she said. "We'll go to the shops tomorrow." Then she turned back and added in a whisper, "My brother was all admiration!"

The next morning Aunt Susan called Elizabeth into her room and gave her a packet of coins. Elizabeth started to protest, but Aunt Susan said, "When you go to the marketplace with Miriam, you will need to get some cosmetics of your own."

"Should I?" Elizabeth asked, reluctantly. "You don't use them."

"No," Aunt Susan agreed with a smile, "and probably you won't after we leave here, but let Miriam enjoy herself. She has never had a little sister, so you are like a doll to her. Besides, you may find gifts to take back to Caleb and Rachel."

Miriam slept late that morning and decided it was too hot to go to the shops when she was finally awake, so they agreed to go early the next morning. Much to Elizabeth's dismay when they got there, Miriam would not let her pay for anything. "Oh, I'm having such a good time," she said. "I want to choose the right eye shadow for you especially, and a blue and gold scarf to go with the gown you wore that first night. Anyway, my father gives me all the money I can use." She giggled. "He wants his family to look rich so his business friends will be impressed."

Elizabeth, however, insisted on paying for a new Damascus knife for her father, and a fine, soft shawl for her mother. There wasn't time to look for anything more.

When they got back, Elizabeth hurried to Aunt Susan's room to show her the purchases and tell her about the day. A servant was just bowing himself out of the room, and Aunt Susan looked upset.

"Is something the trouble, Aunt Susan? Shall I come back later, or is there something I can do?"

"No, no." She smiled with an effort. "Tell me about the marketplace. I must go again. What did you see that would be nice gifts to take back?"

Reassured, Elizabeth opened the net bag she had carried her purchases in and showed Aunt Susan the shawl and the knife, besides the boxes and bottles of cosmetics. She chattered on about the crowds and the shops and the way people were dressed, till she suddenly realized Aunt Susan was only half listening. Casually, she gathered up her purchases. "Now I must hurry to get ready for dinner. Miriam said she wanted to try this new eye shadow on me, and she is going to start showing me how to do it myself. Just wait till you see your charming, painted niece!"

Aunt Susan smiled and nodded. "I can hardly wait," she agreed. But as Elizabeth went quietly out, the smile disappeared.

The next afternoon was so hot Miriam declared she was just going to stay in her room and sleep. Elizabeth found a shady place in the courtyard and sat down to work on the embroidery she had started in Tiberias. It seemed a long time ago. She wondered if Aunt Susan's son was missing them. Gently she smoothed her fingers over the ivory needle box. He had been so kind. Their host, Samuel, who had taken time to show her the ship, reminded her of him. Of course, Miriam's brother, Asher, was younger and more exciting. He was really good looking, too. But suddenly the face in her mind was not Asher's but Nathan's.

The embroidery was lying still in her lap, and she was gazing out over the sea when Aunt Susan found her. Without a word of greeting she sat down on the nearest bench and began in a low voice, "My dear, yesterday you asked me if something was wrong, but I was not yet sure what to tell you. The servant you saw was a messenger from my sister."

Elizabeth's eyes widened, and her face paled. "Nathan?" she whispered.

13

"He is well," Aunt Susan assured her. "He will soon be home, but Hannah sent a message. She thought you should know." Susan was silent for a minute, and Elizabeth hardly breathed till she went on. "Hannah sent me the message Nathan had sent her, and I think the best I can do is repeat it to you. He said for Hannah to prepare to welcome an Egyptian girl he was bringing back. Her maid and her father would be with her. Also Hannah was to send the messenger on to Jeremiah to tell him that the search had been successful and he need make no further offers."

Elizabeth sat like one of the statues around them. The words were there in her mind, but she could not think about them. They were just there.

Aunt Susan sat looking at her. Surely there was no need to add to Elizabeth's shock by telling her the rest of Hannah's message: "How can I welcome an Egyptian daughter-in-law when he might have had Elizabeth?" She reached out to touch Elizabeth's hand, but it was cold and unmoving.

At last Elizabeth began to fold up her embroidery. "Thank you for telling me, Aunt Susan," she said tonelessly. She stood up and added as she walked away, "I will be in my room."

When Miriam came to Elizabeth's room late that afternoon, she found Elizabeth restlessly walking from window to door and back, her eyes red and swollen.

"My dear!" she exclaimed. "Did you sit out in the sun this afternoon? Your eyes are all bloodshot. Sit down here and shut them for a few minutes while I get some eye drops to soothe them." She laughed. "You can't have Asher thinking you're mourning for him because he hasn't been here for a few days. He's conceited enough without that!"

They were a little late for dinner, but Miriam had done an expert job, and Elizabeth looked even more elegant than usual. Asher hurried to take the couch beside her, and as the dinner progressed, he kept them all entertained with stories of his trip to Acre with friends.

Determined not to think of Nathan, Elizabeth laughed with the others and even put in a few comments that made Asher laugh, too. Her face was a little flushed now, and Miriam leaned over to whisper, "Keep him guessing, little sister."

"What secrets are you two hatching?" Asher

demanded in mock anger. "Can't a man be away a day or two without everybody's plotting against him? I'll tell you what—a friend of mine across the city is having a banquet tonight. We don't need food, but let's go for the entertainment. Miriam? Elizabeth?"

Miriam clapped her hands. "Oh, let's. Is it Elihu? He had apes and their trainers the last time we were there. Come on, Elizabeth. You don't mind, do you, Aunt Susan? Asher and I will be with her."

"Apes?" Elizabeth asked. "I've never seen any apes. Where do they come from?"

Elizabeth's eyes had their usual sparkle now, so Aunt Susan smiled. "I'm sure she'll enjoy meeting your friends," she agreed, "but don't keep her out too late."

"Oh, she can sleep late tomorrow," Miriam answered. "We'll take good care of her."

By the time they had finished dessert, a litter had been called for the girls. Miriam and Elizabeth had just stepped in when Asher ordered, "Move over, Miriam. Why should I walk?"

"There isn't room!" she objected, but he was already in.

"Here, you sit on my knees and I'll sit on the seat," he said.

Miriam was laughing as she settled on his lap. "Next time you can hold Elizabeth. I'm sure you'd rather!"

Elizabeth tried to squeeze back into her corner, but it didn't seem to do any good. Asher was close no matter how she sat. By the time they reached his friend's house, she felt crushed and disheveled, but Miriam and Asher were laughing and talking of the people they would be seeing there. Miriam jumped out of the litter with Asher just behind her, but he turned to help Elizabeth down, holding her a little longer to make sure she was steady on her feet. "Are you all right?" he asked in a low voice. "I know it was crowded in there, but I wanted to be near you. Take my arm now, and I'll introduce you to everybody."

If Elizabeth had thought the evening with the family and guests had been crowded, it was nothing to this. Some of the young people were still on the couches by the tables, but others came rushing to greet Miriam and Asher.

"Where have you been?"

"I haven't seen you in ages."

"Asher, introduce us. Where have you been keeping this lovely?"

At first it was exciting, with everybody talking and laughing together. Somebody put a bunch of grapes in Elizabeth's hand, and someone else gave her a glass of wine. In no time, Miriam had settled at a table, but Asher kept Elizabeth near him even when he was talking with all the others. He saw that she had more fruit and made sure her wine glass was refilled.

Finally the host clapped his hands. "Everybody sit in a circle," he directed, "and keep quiet. If you scare the peacocks, they won't display."

"Peacocks!" somebody exclaimed.

"No apes?" Elizabeth whispered to Asher.

The curtains at the side of the room slid open, and a girl in a brilliant blue gown entered, dropping grain from her fingers and holding out her hand with more grain in it. Slowly, a peacock appeared, picking up grain from the floor and then from her hand. The blue feathers on its body were exactly the color of her gown. Turning its head this way and that, the peacock proudly spread its gorgeous tail.

"Oh!" A gasp ran around the circle, as the huge fan opened.

Silently the girl parted the curtains on the other side of the room and glided out, clucking softly to the peacock. Another girl entered from the first side, this one dressed in gold matching that in the circles of her peacock's tail.

And then a third girl entered, in green, but that peacock refused to display no matter how gracefully the girl led him, or how much grain she offered. Finally she shrugged, lifted her arms, and started dancing by herself. The other two girls came back, and the three were soon a whirling, shimmering dance of color.

Elizabeth sat entranced by the dance. She swayed as she watched, as if she could join them. A moment later she saw Miriam and two other girls do just that, weaving in and out, whirling and waving their delicate scarves.

Suddenly the motion made Elizabeth dizzy, and she felt a wave of nausea sweep over her. And then shame. Dancing girls! She'd heard whispers about them. What would her father think of her? What was she doing here?

She stumbled to her feet and tried to think where the door was. Immediately Asher was beside her. "Elizabeth, are you ill? Shall I get you—"

"Take me home," she whispered, swallowing quickly. "Please, please . . ."

"Just a minute. I'll get Miriam." He guided her outside. "Wait here. I'll send for the litter."

She sat down on the stone railing and put her hands to her face. In a few minutes Asher was back. "Miriam doesn't want to come yet. Her friends will see her home."

He helped Elizabeth into the litter. Her head was aching; she felt feverish and sick. Thankfully she leaned against the cool side of the litter, but in a moment Asher's arms were around her and she was leaning on his shoulder.

"I'm sorry to spoil your evening," she whispered.

But he whispered back, "Don't be sorry. You are more beautiful than dancers any day."

She hardly knew when they got home or how she got ready for bed. The next morning her face felt so stiff she realized she had not even taken off the cosmetics.

Elizabeth knew Miriam would sleep late, but she dreaded seeing Asher. She had actually let him put his arms around her! What would he think? She did not see him, though, and later in the day she heard his mother say he had gone to Joppa with friends.

It was a quiet day, and Elizabeth had time to rest and try to think. Did Asher—maybe—care for her? He had brought her home when she asked. Perhaps he would speak to his father. Somehow, she didn't think so. But the peacocks had been beautiful. And she could not have refused to go with Miriam and Asher. Suppose she had been with Nathan? Elizabeth could not imagine it. Or was that where he had found his Egyptian girl? She must not think of him. If she could only talk with Aunt Susan, but she was too ashamed and confused. After all, these were Aunt Susan's friends.

The days drifted by, with Elizabeth and Aunt Susan saying little to one another, each trying to hide her troubled thoughts, and smile when others were near.

At last Asher came back, apparently not even remembering the evening of the banquet. He chatted gaily about his friends and the boat races at Joppa. That evening he announced there were to be horse races in the hippodrome the next day, and he had reserved seats for the whole family. "And Susan and Elizabeth, of course," he added casually.

The next afternoon when they arrived at the hippodrome, Elizabeth looked at the mammoth building in astonishment. It seemed so much bigger than she had thought, now they were close to it. Tiers and tiers of seats rose around the long oval track. "It's almost as big as the temple," she whispered to Aunt Susan.

The older woman nodded, soberly. "But for a very different purpose," she said quietly. "Keep your shawl drawn close around you, child. Even though Miriam's family is with us, there will be people who stare and perhaps jostle you in such a crowd. Keep near me."

Miriam was hurrying carelessly by other people. "Will the white horses that raced last time be here?" she asked excitedly. "The way they ran for that driver was magnificent!"

"The horses or the driver?" her brother teased.

"Oh, you! . . . Elizabeth," she called as they climbed up to the seats reserved for them, "have you ever seen a horse race?"

Elizabeth shook her head. "The Roman chariot horses in Capernaum or Tiberias are the only horses I've seen. But they looked so fierce I kept out of their way."

Miriam laughed as she settled herself. "Well, we're out of their way up here. I like them to look fierce, though. It's exciting."

Elizabeth sat down between Aunt Susan and Miriam, but somehow, as Miriam stood up and turned to wave to somebody, she moved away, and Asher casually stepped in between her and Elizabeth.

They were just in time for the first race. When the

horses started, they were parading beautifully, and their harnesses and chariots shone, but as they came tearing down the track, Elizabeth shrank back. She was glad she was so high up, for it looked as if they would run right into the lower benches. The drivers were hauling on the reins and waving their whips to hold the horses in the right lane. The horses were beginning to froth, with their mouths wide open and their eyes glaring. The spectators were shouting, and some jumped to their feet as the horses passed and went racing around the other side.

"Ooh, aren't they gorgeous?" Miriam squealed, clapping her hands, but Elizabeth shivered, her hands tightly clasped in her lap. The next time they came around, she closed her eyes. She couldn't bear to see the horses whipped to such a frenzy.

"Don't be afraid," Asher murmured, bending over her. "Just lean on me." At the same time Elizabeth realized his arm was around her. For a second, she wanted to turn and hide her face against him the way Caleb would have, but suddenly she stiffened. In public! What was she thinking of? Quickly she turned toward Aunt Susan, and almost at once the arm was withdrawn.

"How did you like it, Elizabeth?" called Miriam, leaning across her brother. "Wasn't it exciting?"

But Elizabeth could not answer. She tried to swallow. What could she say? She must not be rude. Before she could think, Asher began to laugh. "I guess

Elizabeth doesn't think much of our entertainments." Turning to her he asked scornfully, "I suppose you'd rather have a donkey cart race?"

14

ELIZABETH FLUSHED in embarrassment and bowed her head. But then she lifted it again and said firmly, "I guess I don't like any race where the animals are whipped. It could be fun if they just ran because they liked to."

There was a sudden quiet. Then Asher's father behind them said, "Well, I've seen one race, and that's all I have time for. I'll be leaving before the next one. Susan, would you and Elizabeth like to leave with me, or would you prefer to stay with Asher and Miriam and my wife?"

Quickly Aunt Susan stood. "If it will not take too much of your time to see us home, I think we will leave. Thank you, Asher, for helping us see something Caesarea is noted for."

Elizabeth caught the hint. She didn't have to say she had enjoyed the races! "Yes," she said, turning toward Asher but not looking up, "thank you for bringing us here. It will be something to remember." Then she smiled at Miriam. "The hippodrome is a tremendous building, and I'm glad I saw it."

Carefully the three of them stepped down from level to level till they got to the ground, and then they left by a side exit where the donkey litters were waiting. How smoothly he had managed, Elizabeth thought, the way Aunt Susan's son would have. In Tiberias he had come almost every day but never made her feel embarrassed the way Asher did.

When they had settled into the litter Samuel asked, "Do you want to go directly home? Or since the afternoon is early yet, would you care to go out to the aqueducts? They're certainly not as exciting as the races, but I think truly great."

Elizabeth looked up happily, but Aunt Susan hesitated. "Your business—"

"That was just an excuse," he interrupted with a smile. "Those races seem to me such a waste of time when I could be accomplishing something. I know a lot of people enjoy them, but I'll be glad when Asher finds something better to do."

He gave directions briefly to the donkey driver, and they were on their way. As they progressed through the city, he pointed out new homes that were being built, new streets, and big public buildings.

When they came in sight of the aqueduct, he stopped the litter. "See those high, rounded arches?

Those are the supports. Rome builds even practical things with an eye to beauty. Would you like to walk closer?"

He helped them down, and they walked over the sandy beach toward the great structure. Elizabeth lifted her face to the fresh air blowing here outside the city. Through the wide arches she watched the waves of the Great Sea glittering in the sun. At last she smiled and said, "See the waves racing. They chase each other as if they enjoyed it."

Miriam's father nodded. "I never get tired of watching them." He led them a little farther. "There's no way you can get up to see the water in the duct, but come close and put your ear to the pillar. You can feel it rumble like a river."

Elizabeth tried it, then nodded, her face alight. "Like a secret river," she said. Then tipping her head back to look up, she said soberly, "The ones who built it must be very proud." A sudden idea popped into her mind. "Did you?" she asked.

He shook his head. "I'm only a businessman, not an engineer. But I did help raise the money for my city to have this marvel. And yes, I am proud."

Elizabeth nodded. "I am proud you wanted me to see it." They turned and walked silently back to the litter. That evening before she went to bed, Elizabeth crept into Aunt Susan's room and knelt by her.

"What is it, my dear?" Aunt Susan asked, as she laid her hand on Elizabeth's head.

"Would you be very disappointed if we went back to Tiberias soon?"

Susan smiled into the darkness. "Not disappointed at all," she answered. "It's been a long time since we've seen our families." She paused and then went on, "Someday I want to show you Alexandria and other places, but winter is coming, and that's not the best time to travel."

"I'd love to see them, but you've shown me so much already!" Elizabeth responded. "I feel as if I want to think about what we have seen, and then— maybe next year?"

Aunt Susan smiled again. "Maybe next year," she agreed. After a few minutes, she sighed. "I know it is too soon to ask, but do you perhaps think differently now about my son?"

Elizabeth did not speak, but slowly nodded her head. Aunt Susan went on, "It will be second choice for both, but you have grown up in these weeks. Sometimes second choice can be the surest."

Again Elizabeth nodded.

Aunt Susan pulled Elizabeth's face down and kissed her. "Bring your blanket in and sleep by me tonight, child. Tomorrow we will make our plans."

The next day when Aunt Susan told her friends of the plan to leave, they urged her to stay, but she seemed in a hurry to leave once it was decided. Since she didn't want to wait for a chance caravan, Samuel promised two of his servants to ride with them for safety.

Early the second morning Elizabeth packed their clothes and the special things they had bought in the markets: a gold chain for Rachel and a wooden boat for Caleb, besides the things for her mother and father. When she was finished, she went and stood again by the pool in the reception hall, waiting for the time of leave-taking. It was like a dream that she should have been a guest in such a beautiful home and seen so many new places and people.

And yet it would be good to be back home. She was suddenly anxious to see all the family—her father and mother and Caleb. Rachel and Adam. She could picture the whole village in her mind. She would go with Uncle Levi to find the rabbi, Jesus of Nazareth, who had healed Aunt Susan. And Aunt Susan's son— "Jonah," she whispered, trying the name. Would he be glad to see her?

"Elizabeth!"

Not believing the voice she heard, she turned, and saw him standing there. "Nathan!" She ran to him, and he clasped both her hands as they looked at each other in wonder.

"How did you find me? When did you come?" Her joy bubbled up in the little questions that didn't matter.

Suddenly his expression changed. He looked from her face down to her hands. The gladness left his eyes as he stared at the hand he had partly released. He looked back at her face with anger flaring in his. "Why are you wearing a gold ring? You left word Rachel was betrothed, but you didn't say you were. You—you said you would not get tired of waiting. I came as soon as I could!"

He fairly threw her hands down, whirled away from her, and ran through the nearest archway.

Elizabeth stood aghast, staring after him, then down at her hand. Dorcas's ring! How could he think . . . He must listen. She ran past the pillars and looked down the hall. Which way had he gone? She ran to the far end of the hall, but he was nowhere in sight. Oh, why was the house so big?

She stood still, listening for footsteps or voices, trying to think. She could not go into every room. Had he come from Egypt by ship? Had he gone back to the harbor? Elizabeth ran to the back courtyard, but no one was hurrying down the hill. When had he come? Why had no one told her he was here? She pressed her hands to her mouth. She must think.

If Nathan had not come by ship, he must have come right in from the street without anyone seeing him. Had he come by camel and gone first to Jericho? Of course! He had got her message. How else?

Elizabeth ran back through the reception room and out the other way. "Oh, God be thanked," she murmured softly. There was Keva, kneeling calmly on the cobblestones, chewing her cud. He hadn't gone! He could not go without seeing her again, without her telling him. Thoughtlessly she ran toward the camel as if that would bring her nearer to Nathan. Keva, startled, spat her cud and mouthful of saliva at Elizabeth, the whole mess running down the front of her robe.

Elizabeth stopped, horrified. Behind her the familiar voice spoke, this time with amusement. "Did Keva give up her cud for you, my little camel? You are honored!"

She turned slowly and raised her eyes to his, and they both burst out laughing.

Nathan reached out his hands again, but Elizabeth held back. "Please," he said humbly. "I'm sorry. I was so sure, and I came as fast as I could from Jericho, and then I thought . . ." His hands dropped to his side as she frowned, for Elizabeth had had time to remember his mother's message.

Her voice was cold as she asked, "What about the Egyptian girl?"

"What about her?" he asked, puzzled.

"Your mother sent word that you were bringing an Egyptian girl, and your search was ended." Her eyes flashed in anger and humiliation. "How can you come to me when you have just taken your betrothed to your mother?"

"My betrothed! I'm not betrothed! How could I be?" He stopped, thinking back, then went on hesitantly, "Is that why—I thought my mother wasn't as hospitable— what message did I send that she could so misread it?"

"You said Jeremiah need make no further offers."

"So she thought—oh, no! Jeremiah sent me to find a skilled designer and weaver of Egyptian linen and bring him back for the business here. And I did." Nathan's words were fairly tumbling out now. "And of course he had to bring his daughter, since she is unwed and his wife had died. They had no place to come, but I was sure my mother would welcome strangers till they found a home."

Elizabeth's eyes were widening, and the anger was gone, though she still frowned doubtfully.

Nathan took a step toward her. "Elizabeth, I am not betrothed, but I want to be to you. I couldn't stand it when it seemed you were promised to someone else. I thought I was running out of the house, and instead I went stumbling into Aunt Susan's room."

Elizabeth began to smile, and so did he. "She scolded me as if I were a silly little boy. I guess I was. She told me about Dorcas's ring. I'm ashamed, Elizabeth," he went on humbly. "In Jericho I asked my uncle to go to Capernaum and get things straight with your father while I came to you. And now I have tangled everything again."

"And untangled it," she said softly, now holding out her hands.

Eagerly he grasped them. "You shall always wear Dorcas's ring," he promised. Nathan's hands tightened, and his thumb rubbed the ring. "But any other rings you wear, I'll give you, Elizabeth, for the rest of your life."

"I don't need rings," she whispered.

"But you will wear mine?" he asked. "Elizabeth, you will be my wife?"

At last the joy came shining through her face again. "For always," she answered.

And he repeated, "For always."